Unbreakable

Highlands Forever, Book One

Violetta Rand

Print Edition

Published by Dragonblade Publishing, an imprint of Kathryn Le Veque Novels, Inc

BOOKS FROM DRAGONBLADE PUBLISHING

Knights of Honor Series by Alexa Aston

Word of Honor
Marked By Honor
Code of Honor
Journey to Honor
Heart of Honor

Legends of Love Series by Avril Borthiry

The Wishing Well
Isolated Hearts
Sentinel

The Lost Lords Series by Chasity Bowlin

The Lost Lord of Castle Black
The Vanishing of Lord Vale

By Elizabeth Ellen Carter

Captive of the Corsairs, *Heart of the Corsairs Series*
Revenge of the Corsairs, *Heart of the Corsairs Series*
Dark Heart

Knight Everlasting Series by Cassidy Cayman

Endearing
Enchanted

Midnight Meetings Series by Gina Conkle

Meet a Rogue at Midnight, book 4

Second Chance Series by Jessica Jefferson

Second Chance Marquess

Imperial Season Series by Mary Lancaster

Vienna Waltz
Vienna Woods
Vienna Dawn

Blackhaven Brides Series by Mary Lancaster

The Wicked Baron
The Wicked Lady
The Wicked Rebel
The Wicked Husband

Highland Loves Series by Melissa Limoges

My Reckless Love

Clash of the Tartans Series by Anna Markland

Kilty Secrets
Kilted at the Altar

Queen of Thieves Series by Andy Peloquin

Child of the Night Guild
Thief of the Night Guild

Dark Gardens Series by Meara Platt

Garden of Shadows
Garden of Light
Garden of Dragons
Garden of Destiny

Rulers of the Sky Series by Paula Quinn

Scorched
Ember
White Hot

Highlands Forever Series by Violetta Rand

Unbreakable

Viking's Fury Series by Violetta Rand

Love's Fury
Desire's Fury
Passion's Fury

Also from Violetta Rand

Viking Hearts

The Sons of Scotland Series by Victoria Vane

Virtue

Dry Bayou Brides Series by Lynn Winchester

The Shepherd's Daughter
The Seamstress
The Widow

To Kathryn Le Veque for providing the inspiration to go back to the Highlands.

And to DJ, you are like starlight, brightening my life and lighting my pathway to happiness.

Table of Contents

Chapter One

Clan MacKay lands
Northern shore of the Scottish Highlands, 1462

THE WIND CHILLED Alex MacKay as he squinted through the morning mist to catch sight of the lush shoreline where his galley would soon anchor. Years had passed since he'd stood on MacKay lands. He was but twenty then, and convinced he was in love. Betrayal forced him to leave home, and he sold his allegiance, and maybe a bit of his soul, to the princes of Constantinople as a mercenary.

There were no golden palaces decorating the Highland coastline. No bathhouses and perfumed women waiting to welcome him back from battle. No bustling marketplaces where anything a man imagined could be bought. No sand and hot sun. Only gray outcrops and hills, fields of heather and mountains—the very things that breathed life into his battered heart. Things he'd purposely forgotten.

He gripped the missive from his only brother in his left hand, having committed the desperate plea to memory—begging Alex to return home and help defend clan lands from Sutherland raiders.

Did nothing change? Why were Scots so determined to kill each other when the real threats lie south of the border? Squabbling over holdings and sheep couldna compare to the devastation of English swords.

Alex had learned the hard way what real wars were fought over. He'd seen princes dragged into the public square and tortured, hands and feet chopped off, the crowd as bloodthirsty as the executioner. What did MacKays or Sutherlands know of such evil? And deep inside, Alex regretted that he'd ever witnessed such brutality, that he'd ever left the place he once called home. No one would be privy to his regrets, though. Everything that connected him to Scotland, whether family or bitter memories, were locked away in the depths of his soul, along with any feelings he had left.

Soldiers fought with true purpose here, the one thing he appreciated about the men on this side of the world.

After the boat landed, Alex walked up the beach toward a group of waiting horsemen. He immediately recognized the blue and green tartans they wore and the man at the front. Seeing his brother on a massive, black beast was nearly the same as staring at his own reflection in a looking glass. He stopped a few yards away, taking in everything. He'd never imagined being here again, feeling the fine Scottish breeze blowing through his hair or the bite of the salty air on his tongue.

His brother dismounted and quickly closed the distance between them. "Alexander."

"John."

"Ye're here."

In truth, nothing could have kept Alex away. He relished the idea of seeing his brother fail. A man couldna pray for better revenge. He ripped a leather coin purse from his weapon belt and tossed it on the ground at his brother's feet.

"This will pay for the extra swords ye need to protect our sire's holdings."

John sucked in a ragged breath and shook his head. "*My*

lands."

"Call it whatever ye will. I've done my duty. If ye canna manage to hire mercenaries to defeat yer enemy, then ye don't deserve to be laird."

Alex turned back to the water, ready to return to his ship.

"Wait," his brother called. "Ye came all this way just to give me money?"

"No." Alex wheeled around. "I traveled halfway around the world to gaze upon ye a last time."

John's lips drew together. "Why?"

"To see if yer sins have finally caught up with ye."

"That isna an acceptable answer."

"It will have to suffice." Alex was a respected warrior in the exotic lands where he'd carved an existence out with blood, sweat, and some bitter tears. Even the sultans dinna ask for explanations. So Alex would provide none here.

"Ye've been gone five years."

Alex studied his brother's features. The breeze lifted his sandy-colored hair, revealing a long scar along his right jaw. His eyes were creased in the corners and dull. He'd aged hard, which told Alex he'd suffered. "My curiosity is satisfied."

"Dinna speak in riddles."

"Riddles?" he repeated, sounding angrier than he'd intended. "Do I need to spell it out for ye?'

"She's not here."

Bloody bastard dared resurrect that old memory? "Who?" Alex pretended not to know.

"Keely."

Time had dulled the pain, relegating *her* countenance to the occasional nightmare. But the mere mention of her name burned a new hole in his soul. "I doona care." But he did—too much for a man who'd been away so long.

John smirked, acting as if he'd seized the power in their conversation. "Ye're a bad liar."

"Am I?" Alex surged closer, standing a head taller than John. The temptation to beat him senseless nearly won the day. "Ye are the worst sort of thief, *brother.*" There was no love in that designation, no loyalty for his own sibling. Only rage and hatred. Alex touched his sword. In the heat of battle in the desert, he'd often pictured his brother's face as he cut down an enemy. It served a purpose—making him more lethal than most—able to kill a man without caring for who or what he was.

John's shoulders drooped. "She spoke her vows before God but ran away the same night. *Before* we consummated our marriage."

The news did little to ease the hostility swirling inside Alex. His time away had altered his view. The only man he trusted was himself. It kept him alive and made it easier to wake up every day. Men with deeply rooted feelings–a weak man of conscience like John–would have withered and blown away in the desert winds a long time ago. "Good luck," Alex murmured as he turned his back.

"Shame follows ye," John yelled. "Father would roll over in his grave if he knew ye abandoned yer family *again.*"

Though his brother's words reached his ears, nothing touched the black depths of Alex's soul. Numbness ruled him. He must never relinquish the tight control he exercised over his heart. And since he'd grown fond of the silver and gold the eastern princes paid him for protecting their fortresses, he had every intention of returning to foreign shores.

The sound of thundering hooves made Alex stop. Against his better judgment, he looked over his shoulder. A dozen warriors had arrived. He cursed as he backtracked, getting close enough to overhear what they discussed.

"Come now, milord," one said. "There's no time to spare."

"How bad is it?" John asked as he climbed into the saddle, looking more haggard by the second.

"The west village is burning. Many have been killed, I'm afraid."

"The women and children?"

"The Sutherland pigs gave no quarter, milord."

The words *Sutherland pigs* stirred something inside Alex. Memories from his childhood flashed before his eyes—the smell of burning wood, the cries of helpless women seeking their missing children. He'd witnessed Sutherland barbarism too many times as a youth, unable to stand against his enemies because he was too young. Overcome by something powerful, the target of Alex's rage shifted suddenly.

Even the legendary warrior Achilles possessed a weakness. So did Alex. Knowing innocent women and children had been slaughtered lit his blood on fire. John dinna matter. The betrayal of a woman dinna matter. Only the right to live in peace did. And those crofters—people who had served his grandfather and father—deserved his protection.

"What is it, Alex?" John called from his restless steed. "Did Father's ghost whisper in yer ear?"

Alex gazed into his brother's eyes. There was no passion, no thirst for blood vengeance, only a tired man who had been pushed too hard for too long. Perhaps John had missed his calling as a priest, for that's what Alex saw in his elder brother—a man of the cloth, not a man of war. "If Father had anything to say to me, Brother, he wouldna whisper, he'd scream it from the highest peak."

John's warhorse circled him, lifting its front hooves. "There is no time to argue, Alex. Make yer choice. Join us or be on yer way."

Alex unsheathed his curved sword, a gift from one of the princes he'd saved. *"MacAoidh,"* he cried out, identifying himself as a MacKay. The clan motto followed. *"Bi tren…" Be true, be valiant.*

Chapter Two

"WHY AM I weeping?" Keely dismounted, pausing to take in the view of the valley below. She hadn't crossed a MacKay border since her wedding night, abandoning the husband she never wanted, the new laird, John Mackay.

She didn't blame her past on anyone but herself. But after five years of hiding behind the walls of Dunrobin Castle, relying on the charity of the Sutherlands, she'd finally decided to face her past. To seek forgiveness, first from her husband's family, and then her own.

Whether they'd welcome her remained a mystery, for she'd sought sanctuary with the enemy. Which raised the next concern. What name should she use? Keely MacKay, or her father's name, Oliphant? Surely she had no legal claim on the MacKays, for she'd never consummated her ill-fated marriage. Not in the flesh, anyway. However, she had taken vows in the kirk, before her own family, Clan MacKay, and God.

In order to move on with her life, to free herself from the burden of endless guilt, she must attain absolution. Twould be the only way she could show her face in public again.

"Come, Meara." She patted her mare's head affectionately, taking the reins and leading her down the hillside.

The well-worn sheep path would eventually take her to the west village, where the shepherds lived with their families. She missed the bleating of the ewes and lambs, having always been welcomed there.

In the Sutherland keep, she was expected to conduct herself as a lady at all times. There'd been no barefoot walks in the pastures or nighttime swims in the loch. Only sewing and weaving, the occasional ride, and perhaps a bit of music if the laird was in the mood for entertainment. Sutherland women were coddled and kept from the outside world. Unfortunately for Keely, she'd already tasted the sweetness of freedom for too long, so her time there had felt more like a prison sentence.

It had taken many nights of hard riding to evade the Sutherland guards. Keely planned her escape carefully over time, hiding food and clothing in the stables whenever she went riding.

Now, excited to see her friends again, she rode the last couple of miles to the village. What greeted her shocked and saddened her. All that remained of the pleasant cottages were smoldering wood frames and ash.

She slid off her mare and rushed to the closest burned out hut, calling for the women she knew. "Elizabeth? Suzanne? Tara?"

No one answered.

She searched cottage after cottage, hoping to find someone. But everything had been destroyed.

There were no bodies. No signs of violence. Perhaps a cooking fire had been left unattended? Or one of the children accidently set the fire? Regardless of the cause, her heart ached for her friends. A strange feeling settled over her then. For some reason, she could feel the pain and suffering that had happened, and she dropped to her knees and prayed fervently. "Dear God … have mercy on these poor people. On the MacKays. Let whoever did this face holy justice."

"Justice?" a man's voice sounded from behind her. "Ye seek justice in the wrong place, lass. Ye'll find only death and sorrow."

Startled, Keely rose to her feet and found a guard on horseback. "Where are the people?"

He stared at her for a long moment before he spoke again. "Are ye a kinswoman? Did yer ma and da live here?"

She shook her head. "I am a friend. Gone for longer than I ever should've been."

"Tis a bad time to visit, lass. Go home. Violence awaits anyone who comes here."

"Who did this?" she asked.

"Ye ask too many questions. Tell me yer name, lass." He dismounted.

"Keely..." What name should she use? Though she didn't recognize the warrior, he wore the MacKay tartan.

"Yer da's name?"

"I'm Keely ... MacKay."

"The lass who left our laird on his wedding night?"

"Aye," she admitted. "The very woman."

He frowned, studying her. "Ye've heard the news, then?"

"What news?"

"Ye better come with me, lass. It isna safe here."

She hesitated, not wanting to go anywhere with anyone she didn't know and trust. "Who torched the village? Where are the tenants? The animals?"

The guard ignored her questions and retrieved her mare. "Climb up. The answers ye seek will come from the MacKay himself."

"I am more than capable of finding my own way."

"I willna leave a helpless woman here. Especially a MacKay. I have orders and intend to carry them out." He gestured for

Keely to mount.

Living with the Earl of Sutherland had taught her many things. The most important lesson was: once ye cede control, the chance of ever recovering yer independence may never come. On the other hand, she wanted to see her estranged husband. What difference did it make if she arrived with an armed escort or by herself? She sized up the guard, knowing she'd lose the wrestling match if she tried to escape.

"I will accompany ye." She climbed atop her mare. "What is yer name?"

"Andrew," he said, guiding her horse to a spot next to his. "Ye willna protest if I keep yer sweet mare close, will ye?"

A kind way of saying she had no choice. Keely was now in the custody of the MacKays.

Many people watched with curiosity as they entered the inner courtyard of the keep. Before Keely had fled this place, she'd lived amongst the MacKays for over a year. Twas no surprise she recognized several of the women and their now quite grown up children. To say she didn't feel embarrassed and hurt when several turned their backs on her would be dishonest.

She'd expected a cold reception, had even prepared for it, or so she thought.

When the word "traitor" filled the air around her, coming from a single voice first, then growing into a chant, she lifted her hood to cover her face. If they only knew the truth of it, they'd thank her for leaving.

Once a squire took their horses, Andrew escorted her to the great hall. For the time of day, an unusually large number of people were gathered inside. The laird's high table was occupied by what Keely assumed were his captains. The lower benches were also filled with men and some women.

"What is happening?" she whispered to Andrew.

He shushed her. "Listen and learn."

"We canna wait any longer to launch a counter attack," a bearded man at the high table said, pounding his fist on the table for emphasis. "Didn't the good Lord demand an eye for an eye? Well, I propose two Sutherlands for every MacKay that died."

"Bloody cowards," someone yelled from the lower ranks.

"Murdering women and children…" a woman added. "My sons are gone. I canna find my husband."

Sutherlands? What little news from the outside world had reached her ears while in residence at Dunrobin, surely, she would have known if her host was at war with the MacKays. Servants had loose tongues.

"My daughters have been kidnapped." An older woman stood up. "Both of marriageable age, both lovelier than any lasses a Sutherland devil could buy."

The crowd responded loudly, and Keely couldn't keep track of the many conversations going on around her.

"Where is the laird?" she questioned Andrew again. "Shouldn't he be here?"

The answer came when Andrew pulled her aside to make room for the retinue of tartan-clad men to pass by. At first glance, Keely thought John was at the front of the line. But once the light-haired man took the laird's chair at the high table, she realized her mistake.

Though Alexander Joseph MacKay favored his elder brother in many ways, his strong jaw and sharp eyes were unmistakable, even at a distance. She sucked in a shaky breath, her body quaking with fear—even the generous sized hall didn't seem a big enough space for her to share with Alex. The gray stone walls were beginning to close in all around her. She struggled to stay focused.

"What is it?" Andrew gripped her arm. "Ye're as white as an

egg."

"Am I seeing a ghost?" she asked. "Or is that..."

"Settle down," Alex's deep voice penetrated the room. "Speculation willna bring back our kinsmen." He motioned for everyone to sit. Once the room quieted, he continued. "We've captured a half dozen Sutherland warriors. There is no mistaking their clan. But proving a direct link to the earl would be impossible."

"And how did ye reach such a conclusion?" someone asked.

"Logic," Alex offered.

"Logic? Ye've spent too much time with the philosophers in Rome," the man shot back, obviously unconvinced.

Keely heard the men around her snicker.

"True," Alex agreed. "But I've also learned to study my enemy's motives before rushing to judgment. What would the Earl of Sutherland gain from this attack?"

"Satisfaction," the man at the lower table offered.

"A plausible answer," Alex said. "But wouldn't he risk too much by acting so carelessly without cause?"

"The *Battle of Druim na coub* is reason enough. The bastards have waited to avenge their clansmen."

Alex stood and walked around the high table, then stepped off the dais. He approached the man he was speaking to. "Do ye no think I wish the reason were so obvious? Twould be a gift from God to have a justifiable grievance to march outside, climb on my war horse, and ride to Dunrobin at the head of our army—and take back the honor the Sutherlands have stolen from us. Answers to hard questions are rarely found in the open."

"I can name three..."

"I'm listening," Alex said.

"Neil MacKay, Morgan MacKay, and Angus Murray."

Keely knew MacKay clan history well, for her father, Laird Oliphant, had pledged dozens of his own warriors to help defend the former MacKay chieftain from the attack perpetuated by his own cousins thirty-two years ago.

"The Earl of Sutherland dinna ride at the head of his army," Alex pointed out. "He simply took advantage of a situation—pledging some silver and warriors to help stir the shite pot. What better way to defeat an enemy? The eastern princes say *the enemy of my enemy is my friend*, so long as it serves their purpose. The earl wanted the MacKays to destroy themselves."

The room grew eerily quiet.

Keely tried to contain her emotions. But the longer she gazed upon the man she once deeply loved, and the more she heard about the burned village, the more she couldn't stay silent. For she'd lived with the Sutherlands. And if she could aid Alex in any way, to help make up for the pain she caused him by marrying his brother John, she'd do it, no matter the cost.

"Alexander!" She stepped away from Andrew, hoping she'd called his name loud enough for him to hear.

Stormy green eyes met hers. The effect of her presence on Alex became immediately obvious. He squared his shoulders and puffed out his muscular chest.

"Alexander MacKay," she said again, pushing her way to the front of the hall, Andrew at her heels.

His features were stone cold. His lips curled in anger. "Hugh. Bruce. It seems the enemy has penetrated our defenses. Take this woman to a holding cell."

Keely's mouth dropped open in utter shock as her escort, Andrew, latched onto her right arm from behind.

"I begged ye to be still, lass," he whispered. "Tis a bad time to remind the laird's brother of the past. Now I canna help ye."

She turned halfway, able to see Andrew's face. "And why

would ye help me?"

He shrugged. "A lass in need deserves whatever help I can give."

Unsure of his motive, she frowned at him before she whipped around to look at Alex again. He'd only grown more handsome and ruthless, hardened by the life he'd chosen. Or the life she'd forced him into—if she was being completely honest. No Scotsman voluntarily left the Highlands. He must have cause. And she'd given Alex MacKay an endless number of reasons to seek refuge on the other side of the world.

Two red-headed warriors appeared in front of her, the smell of ale and male sweat permeating off their bulky bodies.

"The lass is to come with us," one said to Andrew.

"And where are ye taking her?" Andrew asked, still holding on to her.

"Into the bowels of the keep where she belongs—where all traitors to Clan MacKay end up, before we put them in the ground."

Keely covered her mouth. Surely this was an attempt to frighten her, nothing more.

"Tis no way to talk to a lady," Andrew spat at the towering giants.

"Ye'd oppose a direct order?"

Keely patted Andrew's tense shoulder. He was a man of honor. "Doona risk yer position for me, Captain. I will go with these men."

Hugh and Bruce positioned themselves on either side of Keely, making her feel even smaller and more insignificant than she had before.

As they walked past Alex, he whispered just loud enough for Keely to hear, "Welcome home, Keely."

Chapter Three

HOW HAD THAT blue-eyed she-devil gotten inside the keep? Why now? Alex tried to collect himself, but simply couldn't. He left the great hall—unwilling to show even the slightest crack in his impenetrable façade. Once abovestairs in the laird's solar, he let out the frustrated growl he'd been holding in. So much had happened in the two days he'd been back in the Highlands. If he'd trusted his instincts in the first place, he would have never turned around when he heard the horsemen arrive on the beach. But no, the part of him still in love with his homeland—the side that still swelled with pride whenever he spotted a scrap of blue and green MacKay plaid—overruled the battle-hardened mercenary.

He'd willingly go to Hades before he'd let a Sutherland destroy his family.

"Is she the woman you spoke of?"

Alex eyed the olive-skinned scholar he'd hired five years ago in Italy to accompany him to Constantinople as an interpreter. The man spoke seven languages, including Gaelic.

"Aye," he reluctantly admitted. "What were ye doing in the hall? I asked ye to stay here and cull through the ledgers."

Petro gave him a sad smile. "I cannot fight against my own nature," he said. "I follow the excitement."

"Did ye find what ye wanted belowstairs?"

"I discovered the truth," Petro said. "Now that you have possession of the woman you lost so long ago, what will you do with her?"

Alex raked his fingers through his hair. "Hang her."

Petro's eyebrows shot up. "Is she a spy for these Sutherlands?"

Nothing made sense to Alex. Though the same thought had crossed his mind when he saw Keely. What better way to gather intelligence on yer sworn enemy than to send the very woman who nearly became Lady MacKay? But would she sink to such treachery? Why would she align herself with the Sutherlands against her own clan, the Oliphants? To his knowledge, Keely had always shared a loving relationship with her sire. So the reason she sought refuge with the Sutherlands remained a mystery.

"I doona think her capable of such a thing."

"Then she is not the Jezebel you described."

Alex frowned. "I spoke out of anger."

"You spoke like a man still in love."

There was no room in Alex's life for love. "I love no one."

"Stated by a man whose soul leapt from his body the minute he saw *his* woman."

"Doona try to guess what I'm feeling, old friend. I am flesh and bone like any other man. Of course I feel something deep inside for the girl. But tis not love."

Petro clicked his tongue. "Love is all there is, milord. But who am I to question you? I will return to what I do best." He moved to the table and sat down. "Will you go see her now?"

"Aye," he said. "I canna keep her locked up for no reason."

As soon as Alex descended into the underbelly of the keep, his mood changed with the dismal surroundings. The dungeon was dark and damp. Wall torches provided the only light.

The captured Sutherland soldiers, eight in total, occupied the first two cells, while Keely had been put in the last one. Hugh and Bruce were still with her.

Hugh bowed. "She claims innocence, sir."

"Of course she does," Alex said. "Leave us."

The guards departed.

"Alexander?" Keely appeared from the shadows, gripping the thick metal bars. "Why did ye have me thrown down here like a common criminal?"

The moment he'd dreamt of for five long years was happening. A second chance with the lass he'd always loved. But time changed everything. There would be no sweet words exchanged, no kisses, and surely no lovemaking. He met her gaze. "I will ask the questions, Keely Oliphant."

"Where is John? I demand an audience with my husband."

Alex laughed bitterly. "Husband? How can ye claim that right when ye only fulfilled half of yer matrimonial duties? Did ye not leave him in the middle of the night before he had a chance to sample what pleasures ye had to offer?" His gaze swept over her curvaceous body, taking in every inch of her creamy skin and beautiful face. Time had changed her, too, for the better.

"Tis nothing for ye to worry about."

"Oh, but it is," he disagreed. "Ye've spent these last five years ensconced in the kind of luxury only the Sutherlands can offer. And now the earl has murdered twenty of my clansmen, and eight are still missing."

She sniffled, then reached through the bars. Alex stepped back. "Doona touch me," he rebuked. "Those fingers weave nothing but misery. I'd sooner feel the icy grip of death."

She gasped then, her tears visible in the flickering light. "No crueler words have ever been spoken."

"Blame yerself."

"I deserve yer mockery, Alexander. And I'm prepared to answer whatever questions ye have. Only…"

"Only, what, lass? Did ye think I'd open up my loving arms and take ye back?" His mirthless laughter echoed around them. "I despise everything ye represent. And my brother got little better. He's blood, so I had no choice but to spend time with him."

His heart squeezed a little as he observed her reaction to his scathing words. The tears in her eyes, her defeated posture. Everything about the way she looked and acted demonstrated true remorse. But Alex would leave forgiveness to God. He didn't have time or the desire to exercise mercy. "Ye mean nothing to me or Clan MacKay."

"I don't believe ye, Alex."

He edged closer to the bars. "What would it take to convince ye?"

"L-let me touch ye." She reached between the bars again, her slim fingers inches from his face.

Long ago those fingertips worked magic on his body and soul. Enough to make him want her forever. Enough for him to bend his knee and beg for her hand in marriage. Shaking off what had become a dark memory that constantly plagued him, he pressed against the cold steel bars and encircled her wrist with his hand, tugging her as close as she could get. "Go ahead, lass, touch me where ye will. I am no longer the man ye knew. No longer affected by a pretty face or honeyed words spoken in the heat of passion. Women serve only one purpose for me, and tis not what's between yer ears that interests me anymore."

She struggled to free her hand from his grasp, but he only tightened his hold, giving her a shake.

"Ye're hurting me, Alexander."

He shot a knowing look at her. "Pain makes ye stronger, lass—best ye remember it." He let go, remembering how he'd left the Highlands in the middle of the night after she broke his heart, too ashamed to even bid his father farewell. He'd sailed to the Orkney Islands first, then joined several men who were bound for Constantinople in search of fame and fortune.

In reality, he should thank the lass for sparing him a lifetime of wedded misery. Her betrayal provided him with the opportunity he needed to carve out his own existence—to earn his own money. By Highland standards, Alex MacKay was a wealthy man—he could afford to buy a title of his own, even start his own clan.

"Where is John?"

Alex gritted his teeth. Every time the lass spoke, it felt as if he'd been dragged through hot coals, his body on fire with a litany of dangerous emotions. Honestly, dreams couldna compare to seeing Keely in person again. Though he disliked her, she did appeal to his carnal side still—like smelling the soft fragrance in her hair or feeling the heat that radiated from her tiny body. He silently thanked the heavens for the steel barrier between them; otherwise, he'd show her how he truly felt.

"Alexander..." she said. "I want to see John. Now."

His mouth fell in a tight line. Who was she to make demands of any kind? A spoiled Sutherland wench? Rage took over, and he ripped the skeleton key from his belt and unlocked the cell door.

"Ye want to see yer *husband*?"

"Aye."

"I willna keep ye from him any longer, then." He pulled her out of the cell and gripped her arm. "Say nothing to me, Keely, or I'll shove ye back in that cell so quickly, yer teeth will rattle."

Alex kept a firm grip on her arm as he directed her up the

stairs, down a long corridor, then outside. They crossed the inner courtyard to the kirk.

"Ye requested an audience with John, milady?"

She nodded.

Her audacity was admirable. Keely never shrank from speaking her mind or letting her feelings be known. In another lifetime, she would have made a formidable wife for a laird.

Letting go of her arm to open the heavy wooden door of the kirk, he stepped aside to grant her access. The sanctuary was bathed in candlelight. A table stood at the center of the nave, surrounded by silver candle stands and decorated with heather wreaths.

Keely gaped at Alex. "Why are we here?"

"Go." He gave her a shove. "Look for yerself."

He watched with fascination as her curious gaze swept the open space. Twas time someone taught the infuriating lass a hard lesson—*be careful what ye ask for.*

Keely inched closer to the table. Lying in repose and draped in MacKay plaid with his sword gripped in both hands, was Laird John MacKay.

He'd fallen in battle yesterday. The memory was so real—Alex had fought back-to-back with his brother; they were outnumbered by the Sutherland soldiers. It dinna matter, for together, Alex and John were invincible—united by their love for Clan MacKay.

Alex fought lightning-quick and without mercy, while John could deflect any blow. Once they'd cleared the area around them, John pointed to three of his men who seemed to be struggling to defend their ground.

Alex scanned the field. "There's another skirmish over there."

"Aye," John said. "But Mathe is with them. The others need our guidance more."

Alex nodded and raised his sword. "Go!"

Within moments, an arrow shot by a coward hidden within the trees struck John in the back. By grace alone, Alex caught his brother before he fell.

"God damn all Sutherlands," Alex said, positioning John's head on his lap.

John struggled to take a full breath but managed a weak smile. "The Sutherlands breed like rabbits—twould take a lot of damning to get them all." He coughed up blood.

Death eventually claimed every man, and Alex could sense it in John already. Like a flickering flame, the faraway look in his brother's eyes meant one thing. "Let me get the bastard that shot ye in the back."

"Nay." John gripped Alex's hand, holding firmly. "Stay with me, Brother. I doona want to die alone."

"Ye're no dying," Alex lied.

John snorted. "Ye canna always be right."

"I can." Alex looked over his shoulder, then left and right to make sure there were no Sutherlands left unchecked.

"Promise me..." John squeezed his fingers. "Doona leave again. Stay. Claim the lairdship."

"Ye're Laird MacKay, not me."

"Alex!" John closed his eyes.

"I'm here."

"I'll have another oath from ye." John gazed up at him.

"Anything." Another lie.

"Doona let them burn my body as Da did. Bury me in the kirk as is fitting for a laird. With my sword and shield—wearing my plaid and boots. I'm a bloody Highlander, not a fooking Viking."

For the first time Alex could remember, the sting of remorse hit him—tears gathered in the corners of his eyes, but he swallowed that pain. He'd not let his brother see him cry like a woman or bairn. Never. "Aye," he said, admiring John in that moment—not only for his bravery but for his words. "Whatever ye wish.'

"Alex!" John called again. "I see Ma. Da."

No. Alex wouldna let him go. "Stay with me," Alex whispered.

But it was too late. John took a rattling, shallow breath and dinna move again.

Alex closed his brother's eyes and gently lifted his head off his lap. That regret instantly turned into something the devil would claim—an insatiable need to slaughter Sutherlands. And when he killed the two in sight, he'd seek more out.

Keely's guttural cry brought Alex back to the present and pierced his heart. But he'd not give her the satisfaction of seeing the pain and regret on his face.

"How?" she sobbed, kneeling beside the husband she'd never claimed. "When did he die, Alex?"

"Yesterday."

"If I'd only known Earl Sutherland was…"

"What?" Alex spat. "What would ye have done?" He moved closer.

"Saved him."

He laughed. "Tis partly yer fault he's dead."

Keely wobbled to her feet and faced him. Her eyes were swollen, her cheeks stained with fresh tears. "How dare ye blame me for his death. I havena seen nor spoken with this man since the night I left. Call me anything ye wish, curse me, hate me … but don't ye ever say something so evil again. Tis true I never loved him, Alexander, but I respected him enough to leave before I broke his heart."

So beautiful … so unbelievably self-righteous in her darkest hour. "Mourn the husband ye so conveniently claim when it benefits ye greatly."

He headed for the door, not wanting to spend another moment alone with her.

"Alex…"

He stopped, but dinna turn around. "Aye?"

"When are ye going to mourn the brother ye forgot?"

"When Hades freezes, woman."

Chapter Four

DEAR GOD, ALEXANDER... Her heart clenched. What had started as a journey of absolution had turned tragic. She'd never considered seeing Alex again. He'd abandoned his home on the morning of her wedding. Sinking to her knees, Keely tried to forget the past, but couldn't. On the eve before her wedding, Alex had sought her out in her bedchamber. Knowing the danger if they were caught together, she'd begged Alex to leave. Of course, he refused, barring the door and demanding answers.

"Do ye know what ye're doing to me, lass?" he'd asked.

What about her own heart? Had he ever considered what she was feeling? Keely searched his face for the answer, but only found resentment in his eyes.

"Tis the only time I ever remember ye not being able to speak."

"P-please go, Alex."

"Are ye in such a hurry to be rid of me?" He scrubbed his stubbled chin. Usually clean shaven and dressed with care, the man standing before her resembled an outlaw, unkempt, his plaid a wrinkled mess. "A few nights ago, ye were in my arms, promising ye'd be mine—kissing me wildly, begging me to claim ye." He advanced, backing her into the stone wall. "Give me hope, Keely—just a scrap of it and I'll wait a lifetime for ye..."

Oh, that she could... But silence was the price of her future happiness, that and giving up the only man she'd ever love. "What lass wouldna beg for ye to claim her?" Keely asked. "The devil has blessed ye with charms hard to resist."

He chuckled mercilessly, fingering a strand of her dark hair. "Then surrender to those charms, lassie—yer heart will follow after I've loved ye."

Unable to escape, Keely hugged her middle protectively, a meager attempt to keep his roving gaze from noticing how hard her nipples were, wishing her nearly transparent chemise was a cloak of thick wool and fur. "I must go to yer brother's bed a maiden."

Alex seethed, pointing his finger at her. "Aye," he confirmed, "Ye'll go to his bed a virgin, but get a cold reception, for I'll run my sword through his worthless heart." Alex thumped his chest. "Ye betrayed me, lass. Sold yer soul to a man with a title, nothing more."

Keely closed her eyes, grieving her loss, unable to tell him what she really wished to say. Suddenly she was being tugged away from the wall. Opening her eyes, she met Alex's dark stare as his mouth slanted over hers, his strong hand cupped at her nape, forcing her to accept his kiss. A cruel kiss, meant to dominate and remind her of who she really belonged to.

Keely didn't need reminding as their tongues swirled together in anger and desperation, his scent overwhelming her senses, his taste as pleasant as ever.

"That's right, lass," he whispered against her parted lips. "See how easily ye open up to me." He pumped his hips, pressing his hard length against her belly. "Feel what ye do to me."

She planted her palm on his chest, intending to push him away. Instead, she savored the hard muscles she felt through his shirt, unable to ignore the feel of his thundering heartbeat against her fingertips. This was what true love and passion was supposed to feel like. Tears stung her eyes then, but she swallowed her cry. Sacrifices must be made, sometimes, even if what she was expected to give up meant everything in the world to her.

She gazed up at Alex, wanting to commit his face to memory—from his brilliant green eyes, to his narrow, straight nose, to his full lips. No man had ever caught her attention the way Alex had. Nor had she ever desired another man. "Leave me." It wasna a request.

As if something had suddenly come over him, Alex shoved her away, growling with anger. "Ye're not worth the trouble," he spat. "Ye reek of betrayal, the vile taste upon yer once sweet lips and tongue."

She said nothing as Alex stormed toward the door and punched the wall.

"Curse ye, woman, and all who serve ye."

Crushed by the five year-old-remembrance that felt as if it had only happened yesterday, Keely returned her attention to the present, to John. Using the edge of the table as leverage, she raised herself up, her legs still wobbly.

"I came here to beg forgiveness, John." She stared down at his face, reaching for his cheek. Cold to the touch—her husband-in-name-only appeared to be sleeping, even though she well understood the finality of death. "I wish ye peace. Love. Happiness in the heavenly realm—for I know no other man who deserves it more than ye."

Laird John MacKay had always been kind to her. Willing to let her wait to consummate their marriage. She bowed her head, remembering his words—the ones he'd spoken after he'd carried her to their bedchamber on their wedding night.

"Ye canna force love, lass. And I willna do so with ye, though every part of my being craves ye like a madman."

She'd thanked him for his generous consideration and crawled into bed still wearing her gown and slippers, too afraid to undress in front of her new husband. Instead of joining her, John poured himself a cup of wine and sat in a chair in front of the hearth, drinking himself to sleep on what should have been one of the happiest nights of his young life.

Once his light snore was heard, Keely crept from their bedchamber. It had taken every bit of courage she could muster to leave what promised to be a union filled with mutual respect and admiration. For no other man in the Highlands would have given her the gift of time like John. Not even Alex—who she loved with all her heart. Nay, Alex would have claimed her, and she would have offered herself like a sacrificial lamb, married to him or not.

Easier than she thought it would be, she crept past the revelers in the great hall and ran to the stables. Not a squire or stable lad was in sight. Everyone had been invited to her wedding celebration, high and lowborn. She found her mare in a stall in the back of the stable, and with the skill of a seasoned soldier, saddled her mount, then secured her only bag before she climbed up.

Once she was outside, Keely pulled her hood up and looked about. Soldiers were always on patrol. She leaned forward and patted her mare's neck. "If we doona leave now..." She heeled the beautiful horse her sire had bought her a year ago in the ribs. "Go."

Once she finished with John, Keely approached the chancel, the sacred area of the kirk reserved for the priest. Sitting atop the wood altar was a gold cross. How she wanted to take it in her hands and weep. Considering herself unworthy of touching the holy relic, she simply admired it.

"Tell me what to do, Lord. Direct my hands. Speak to my heart. Please..."

When no answer came, she returned to the table where her husband rested. She covered John's big hands with hers, wishing she could breathe life back into his body.

"I am sorry, milord," she sobbed. "Sorry I never gave ye the chance to love me. Sorry I dinna explain myself before I ran away. Sorry I ever met yer brother that day near the loch. I wonder where we'd be now if fate hadn't brought us together."

She leaned over the table and placed a tender kiss on John's lips.

"Judas kissed the Lord before the Sanhedrin guards arrested him in Gethsemane."

She closed her eyes and tried to place the man's voice.

"Lady Keely," the priest said as he came to stand on the

other side of the table. "Some of the women told me I would find ye here."

"Father Michael," she said, feeling uncomfortable in his presence. The priest had presided over her wedding. "If ye doona want me here..."

"Tis not my choice to make," he said. "God calls his children home at the most inconvenient times. But his wisdom is greater than my own. So, I accept ye, child."

"Ye've shown me more mercy than any of the MacKays."

"Did ye expect to be welcomed as a long-lost friend?"

Keely stepped back from the table and licked her dry lips. "I dinna know, Father."

The priest rested his hand on John's forehead. "I've outlived the sire, and now his first-born son. What future awaits this clan?" He whispered a blessing and then invited Keely to follow him to a wooden bench. "Sit," he said.

She scooted to the far end and folded her hands in her lap.

"I will ask the same question I am sure everyone is thinking when they see ye. Why did ye return?"

She should get up and walk away. Arguing with Alex was one thing, but revealing her deepest secrets to a priest was like playing with fire. There would be no half-truths shared in the presence of God or her dead husband. Today must mark the beginning of her new life. "To seek absolution," she confessed.

"From who?" He rubbed his chin.

"From John." She gazed in the direction of the table. "But it seems I am too late."

"Anyone else?"

"God."

"A prayer offered from any kirk would have gained the Almighty's forgiveness."

"Perhaps," she said, not completely in agreeance. Her eyes

grew hazy again as tears gathered in the corners of her eyes. "Cowards hide from the past. Twas only right to come back here."

"Ah," he uttered. "But cowards also run away from their responsibilities."

She knew what he was implying, and though she didn't like it, she couldn't deny his words. "There is no excuse for what I did. But please remember, Father, I was very young. Sixteen."

"I've presided over the marriages of lasses not a day over thirteen."

Keely knotted the material of her skirt between her hands. "I doona doubt it, Father Michael. But for me, it wasna the right time or with the right man."

He swallowed, never taking his gaze off her. "I admire yer courage, lass. But the laird is gone. Rest easy, yer past will be buried with him."

"But not my heart."

"Nay," he said. "Ye will have to live with that for a long time."

Finished with the confession, she stood. "Thank ye for speaking with me."

"Where will ye go, Keely?"

She shrugged, feeling very much alone. "I canna return to Dunrobin. My association with the Sutherlands is forever severed after what I've seen here today."

"A wise choice."

"If my sire will take me..."

"Would it help if I sent him a missive explaining how sincere ye've been—how sorry ye are for running away?"

"I don't regret running away, Father. I'm sorry for the way it happened, though. There's a distinct difference."

"I'm well aware." There was an intensity in his gaze she

hadn't noticed before. "Would ye indulge an old man and confide in me why ye dinna stay with John?"

She cleared her throat and tried to find the strength to answer. "B-because I never loved him."

He nodded in understanding. "Who did ye love, lass?"

"No one." Had she just lied again? Before a priest and on consecrated ground? "Forgive me, Father Michael. Fear once again overrode my sense of truth. Twas Alexander MacKay I wanted and loved, not John."

Father Michael patted her hand. "Ye are forgiven. Under the circumstances, the truth matters not, for ye have no place here now. Yer only connection to Clan MacKay will be buried with Laird John tomorrow. Go in peace, Lady Keely. I will pray for a successful reunion with yer sire."

She curtsied, determined to leave the MacKay stronghold before the sun set.

KEELY LOVED ME? Alex had never left the sanctuary. Instead, he hid in an alcove and listened to everything she said. Her words did nothing to change his mind about her. In fact, it made him distrust her even more. For if she'd truly loved him, why did she pledge herself to John?

As he strolled away from the kirk, he shook his head. Women were capricious creatures. He'd never let another beautiful face manipulate him. He'd never believe another woman's sweet lies or open up his heart to one. Plenty of foolish men would, but Alex refused to be counted among them.

Tomorrow he'd bury his brother and oversee the election of a new laird. As long as a MacKay sat upon the chieftain's chair, he cared little about what happened afterward. He'd already done more than he'd ever planned by staying to defend his clan against the Sutherlands.

His galley awaited his return—as did the princes of the far east. In the land of Mohammed, infidels were free to do as they liked, so long as they didn't curse the Prophet or Allah. Alex could live with those stipulations more than he could live in this place where too many ghosts haunted him.

"Milord." Jamie joined him in the courtyard. "Some matters need yer attention in the great hall."

"I left ye in charge, Jamie. We are kinsmen, and it's my intention to put yer name before the council to elect ye as the next chieftain."

Jamie came to a dead stop. "Me? Laird?" He shook his head. "The council convened while ye were out."

The news pleased Alex. The less they relied on him to solve their problems, the better the chances of this branch of Clan MacKay surviving. "And what did they decide?"

"Tis better for all of the council members to speak for themselves."

"Every warrior has the right to vote, Jamie."

"Aye," he said. "Several names were put before the council."

"And?"

Alex followed his tight-lipped cousin into the great hall. The only other time he'd seen such a showing of blue and green plaid was on the battlefield. As he approached the high table, the men stood.

"Be seated," he said. "Formality isna required here. We are all MacKays."

"But not all of us are lairds," Craig, one of his brother's captains, pointed out.

"I'd prefer to wait until John is in the ground before we choose the next chief. But under the dire circumstances, I understand yer need to take a vote."

"There's no need, milord," Craig said.

Alex sat down, looking into the crowd. "Why?"

"We already voted," Jamie said.

"Without me? I dinna have a chance to vote."

"Yer choice wouldna matter, Alex," Craig said. "The decision was unanimous."

"All right." Alex would listen to what they had to say. These men would be left to hold together whatever remained of his family, so their opinions mattered more than his.

"Before God and all men representing Clan MacKay, we pledge our lives to our new laird." Mathe, the eldest and highest ranked captain of the bunch, pushed his chair out and knelt before Alex.

Jesus Christ above... This was the last thing Alex expected or wanted. He wasna meant for the laird's seat, and dinna deserve it after being gone so long. If these honorable men knew what had taken root in his heart since the night he fled home, they'd surely change their minds about him. There was more to being a laird than just carrying the blood of his sire and brother. It required patience and judiciousness, a healthy fear of the Almighty, and respect for men less fortunate than himself.

All characteristics Alex admired in other men, but was sure he dinna possess himself.

"Stand before me as an equal, Mathe." Alex gestured with his hand. "Venerate a man worthy of the title."

The captain did as he asked but looked confused. "Ye are our choice—which makes ye worthy of the honors."

"Nay," Alex said firmly. "In order for me to be laird, I must live here. I have no intention of staying in the Highlands."

A loud murmur rose from the crowd below.

"Tis no coincidence ye showed up when ye did, Laird Mac-

Kay," Mathe continued, talking louder so the rest of the people in the hall could hear everything he said. "Only God can be credited with such timing."

"Or the devil," Alex murmured.

His words caused more unrest.

"Are ye no a Godfearing man?" someone questioned from the crowd.

"Would ye abandon us again?" a woman cried.

"If ye dinna want to stay, why'd ye defend us against the Sutherland dogs?" another man asked.

Alex sighed and crossed his legs under the table. All fair questions. Their fears and uncertainty were justified, for the future of Clan MacKay was at stake. Standing, Alex raised his hands. The least he could do was try to provide some comfort and leadership until the next laird was chosen. "I am not the man ye think I am," he said. "I'm a sellsword, a bloodthirsty, soulless creature who kills for a living."

Silence settled over the great hall.

"The blood of other men has paid for the properties I own in Constantinople. I keep six concubines, who I bed without hesitation for the sake of pleasure alone. I no longer pray to God for mercy and understanding. I wake each day wondering who I will be sent to hunt and kill. No one calls me friend, but all seek my approval out of fear that it's their throats I will cut next. Is this the type of laird ye want?"

"Ye keep slaves?" Jamie asked, looking shocked.

"Aye," Alex admitted. "And I am a better master than most."

"Tis an abomination," Ramsey MacKay, another cousin and a captain in John's personal guard, commented, his face twisted with disapproval. "But a forgivable one considering where ye've been. Living with heathens so long has caused ye to stray from the ways of God. But even the prodigal son was welcomed back home after living a life of sin."

"I appreciate yer understanding, good cousin—even yer attempt to explain my misdeeds. But I assure ye, I am not easily misled by anything or anyone. I live as I do freely, and without regret."

"Are the lassies more beautiful than ours? Is that what keeps ye away?" an old woman asked.

The men sitting at the high table laughed.

"If that was the only reason, I'd bring my concubines with me," Alex assured her.

Just as he was about to continue explaining himself, Keely entered the great hall. Unable to keep his eyes off her, the crowd followed his wandering gaze.

"There's the reason Alex MacKay willna stay," the old woman yelled, pointing at Keely. "Keely Oliphant broke his wee heart."

Several men standing in the back of the room advanced on Keely, cursing her name and presence.

"Cut her throat," one suggested. "End the laird's madness..."

Instinctively, Alex unsheathed his curved sword and dashed through the crowd, trying to reach Keely before anyone hurt her. But before he could get to her, someone had already shoved her out the door.

Chapter Five

THREE STRANGERS TRAPPED Keely between them and forced her outside. One of the men stopped her, and started to bind her hands with a length of rope he yanked from around his waist.

"Nay!" Keely twisted her hands free. "Let me go!"

But the other two men quickly gripped her upper arms, forcing her hands in front of her again.

The women in the courtyard stopped sorting the fruit and vegetables or washing their clothes, and even the men abandoned their horses and joined her captors, rallying around them, happy to condemn Keely to Hades. With her hands tied together, she couldn't defend herself against someone who threw a piece of fruit at her. She was hurried to a far corner where a platform stood. She recognized the place from when she used to live here. Whenever the laird wished to publicly punish an offender, he was taken to the stage, tied to the post, and either whipped or executed.

"Climb the stairs," one of the men holding her commanded, "Or I'll drag ye up."

Eyeing the stage, she struggled to get away, but was quickly shoved forward. She stumbled and fell to her knees.

"Try to escape again and I'll take what dignity ye have left."

"Do ye know who I am?" she asked the dark-haired man

who dared to mishandle her.

"Aye." He spat on the ground. "Lady Keely Oliphant, the daughter of the laird himself. But yer title makes no difference to us. Ye are the reason Laird John refused to marry, again, or even sire a bastard. And ye're now the reason Alex MacKay refuses to accept his responsibility as the new laird."

Lifted to her feet, Keely had no choice but to amble up the wooden stairs. As she turned around to face the growing throng, a rock hit her in the arm, another on the chest. She swallowed the pain down, raising her chin defiantly. She'd not give them the satisfaction of knowing how she really felt—that deep inside she'd known this moment was coming.

Clan MacKay might not be the wealthiest, but their pride and fierce loyalty was known throughout the Highlands, making them a well sought-after ally. That Alex's people would wish her dead after all these years came as no surprise. Another rock barely missed her face. Her heart skittered. Where were Alex and the captains of the guard? Surely this violence wasn't sanctioned by the council or anyone else in power. She searched the back of the crowd, hoping to find someone to help her.

"On yer knees, harlot." The dark-haired man forced her down. "Our laird is dead. Justice is left to us…"

"Whip her good, Angus," several people howled in unison.

"This woman promised herself to one brother, and then married the other," Angus continued, only to be drowned out by more angry calls.

"Whore!" a woman spat.

"Sutherland spy!" a group of men called.

"Kill her. Blood for blood!"

Keely bowed her head, fear slowly overwhelming her sense of control. Why had she been so foolish and left the safety of Dunrobin Castle? At least the Earl of Sutherland, his sons, and

Helen, the earl's only daughter, treated her as family. She'd lacked for nothing … except freedom. That thought forced her to look up again, into the faces of the people so quick to punish her.

"Confess yer sins, woman, and I might be convinced to show mercy."

"What sins?" Keely asked. "Those of a confused, young lass?"

Angus raised his hand and slapped her hard across the face. The sting brought tears to Keely's eyes. "What say ye now?"

"Violence will change nothing," Keely stated resolutely. Only Father Michael and God had the right to judge her—maybe Alex—for it was his heart she'd broken. But not…

A knife sailed past Keely's cheek. Thrown from the side of the platform, the weapon landed deep in Angus's chest. Keely screamed as her captor faltered, blood seeping from the wound.

"The next man or woman to raise a hand against Keely Oliphant will feel the bite of my blade, too."

It was Alex, in all his rage and glory. He climbed onto the stage, taller and stronger than the other two men who had taken her outside.

"This is the way ye treat the daughter of an old friend—a noblewoman?"

Fear reached the men's eyes as they dropped to their knees, groveling before Alex—the way they'd expected her to do when threatened with death.

"Forgive us, laird, we were only doing what we thought best for ye and the clan."

Alex made a scoffing sound, sickened by their excuse. "Jamie. Marcus. Take these men below. Maybe a few nights in a bloody cell will open their eyes."

"Aye, Alex." Jamie joined him on the platform, followed by

several other guards.

Then Alex turned to the stunned crowd. "I count at least fifty of ye. Fifty heads to decorate the spikes I'll plant along the southern wall of this keep to warn any would-be rebels of the price they'd pay for hurting a hair upon Lady Keely's head."

The throng instantly dispersed, leaving only a handful of guards below, and Alex and Keely on the stage. Unsure what to do, Keely gazed up at him. His shoulder-length, blond hair whipped in the wind. "Thank ye."

"Doona be too quick to thank me, Lady Keely." He scooped her into his arms and carried her down the stairs. "Seems I canna let ye go. Though our intimate bond is forever severed, I canna risk yer life. Until I can arrange for ye to be safely delivered to yer father's house, ye will remain here."

When he kept walking with her in his arms, Keely wiggled uncomfortably. "Put me down."

He ignored her demand and kept moving.

"Alexander MacKay!"

He didn't even look at her.

"Laird MacKay, please set me on my feet, I am capable of walking. And if ye would be so kind as to cut my hands free…"

His lips twitched as he finally met her gaze. "Ye're in no position to make demands, lass."

She couldn't believe it. Why would he prefer carrying her over letting her walk? And why wouldn't he untie her hands?

"If yer wondering why I choose to carry ye inside, tis a show of protection for all to witness. As for the hands, lass, I'll free ye when I'm convinced ye'll stay where I tell ye to."

ALEX DIDN'T MISS the disapproving looks of his clan as he hurried through the great hall. Apparently, they hadn't forgiven Keely for what she'd done to him or John. Such shame and humiliation never faded. He knew it all too well, and now that she was in his custody, Alex's imagination was getting the best of him by formulating a hundred different ways he could make her suffer for wounding him so deeply.

Shuffling up the stairs with her snugly in his arms, he arrived at the bedchamber he'd chosen for her. He set her down, and Keely stared at him, a peculiar look on her face.

"Are ye unwell, lass?" He'd not considered her feelings before, how hopeless she must have felt with Angus.

She shook her head. "Why this bedchamber?"

He opened the door, and she followed him inside. "Tis the most comfortable in the keep, my…"

"Yer mother's room. I remember. How long did I occupy this chamber?" She wandered to the hearth, running her fingers over the tapestry hanging above it. "The last thing yer mother ever made. Tis beautiful, Alex." She turned around and offered a sad smile. "It captures the lushness of Clan MacKay lands—the heather-strewn fields, the north wall of the keep, even the loch."

"Aye," Alex agreed, leaning against the closed door, his arms folded over his chest. "My ma loved this place."

"I'm sorry, Alex. I dinna mean to dredge up old memories."

He slowly smiled at her, chuckling sarcastically. "Nay? Yer return makes me doubt that very much." She was a walking, talking bad memory, the kind that would crush a weaker man's spirit. But Alex wasn't defenseless anymore—that's what he kept telling himself.

She fell silent and turned back to the hearth. "I doona blame ye for being suspicious. My heart is truly broken over everything that's happened—especially John's death."

"Is it?" Why would she care whether his brother lived or

died? Whether his clan thrived or failed? She fled Clan MacKay in the middle of the night, taking his heart and John's with her.

"What do ye mean?"

"Are ye a spy for the Sutherlands?"

She squinted at him, her full lips forming a hard line. "The Earl of Sutherland is an intelligent man, Alex. Why would he send me to do his bidding when he has hundreds of men at his disposal?"

"I told ye I'd ask the questions, lass."

"I remember."

"It would serve ye best to listen."

"Or what?" She stepped away from the hearth, eyeing him with cool interest.

"Are ye a spy?"

"Jesus have mercy..." She rolled her eyes. "I know I took ye by surprise. Imagine how I felt coming back here to speak with John and finding ye instead. Had I known ye were here, I would've stayed away."

"The feelings are mutual, lass, believe me."

"I am no spy, Alex. Just a woman who wishes to reunite with her family."

Was she daft? If she wanted to go home, why'd she ride so far northwest? Her sire's lands were in the opposite direction. "Did ye forget where yer da lives? Twould have been a much shorter journey to yer home."

She huffed out a frustrated breath. "I am not stupid, Alex MacKay. And I have a keen sense of direction. My intention was to gain John's forgiveness first, and maybe even an annulment before I faced my father."

"Annulment?" So she could reclaim her life and find happiness with another man? He strode across the room, angry that she'd even suggest it. "John wouldna have agreed to such an arrangement. The MacKay's are a proud clan, Keely."

"Annulments are common enough."

"Not to the MacKay's."

"I doona understand?"

Alex stared at the woman like he'd never met her before. "An annulment suggests failure, Keely."

"My failure, not John's."

"Spoken like a woman who doesna understand what a man is made of—what drives him."

Keely blinked at him. "Aye, I understand. Ye call it pride and honor, but I consider it pigheadedness."

Alex pumped his hands closed several times, hoping to alleviate some of the building pressure in his chest. The she-devil had openly insulted him. "Pigheadedness?" he repeated as he stepped even closer to her. "Ye destroyed John's life."

"Aye, I played a part in his misfortune, but so did ye."

Almost forehead to forehead, he gazed down at her, not missing the spark of anger in her fathomless eyes or the soft fragrance in her hair. Keely Oliphant might represent everything he wanted to forget, but she was still the most beautiful woman he'd ever seen. Which only made his rage run that much hotter, for she once belonged to him. "Be careful where ye point yer finger, lass. I played no part in yer deception. If anything, I am the unluckiest of all. Ye promised yerself to me, then went behind my back and accepted my brother's offer for marriage."

"We were young," she said.

"Ye were wanton, Keely. Ready to surrender that maidenhead to me." He reached for her hands and she flinched. Why? In his experience, women who winced like that were victims of abuse. *Has someone hurt her?* Regardless, he pulled the twine off, freeing her. "Ye were mine."

She retreated a step, rubbing her wrists. "I belong to no

man."

"Every female on God's green earth belongs to a man, lass. Whether her sire or husband, brother or uncle, doesna matter."

Very slowly she raised her head and met his gaze. "What do ye want from me, Alex?"

Alex curled his fingers under her stubborn chin, turning her face side to side. "I doona know yet, lass. But until I do, ye're to stay here." Satisfied he'd made his wish clear, he turned on his heel and headed for the door.

"Alex?" she called.

He dinna stop until he was in the hallway with the door shut. Curse God for bringing her back into his life. In the short amount of time he'd been back in the Highlands, everything that had happened gave him every reason to want to leave. He only needed to ride for the beach where his ship waited to take him home. Twenty of his best warriors were with him, men who had pledged their allegiance to him in Constantinople. Men he trusted more than anyone.

He closed his eyes and imagined he was back in the desert, riding one of his stallions through the endless sand dunes, nothing on his mind but speed and freedom. That world seemed more like a fantasy now. "Damn this place." He stormed off, ready to drink himself into oblivion.

Chapter Six

AFTER A SHORT time, hoping Alex had other duties to attend to and was gone, Keely risked opening the door to her chamber. There was so much commotion going on belowstairs, she hoped to slip away unnoticed. After all, she'd done so before, in the middle of a wedding feast. No one wanted her here. If someone did see her, why would they alert the guards? The sooner she left, the better for Clan MacKay.

But much to her disappointment, two guards were posted in the corridor.

"Lady Keely," one said. "What do ye need?"

"I-I…" she struggled for an excuse. "Food. Water for a bath. Please."

"Laird MacKay has already seen to yer comfort, milady. A lass from the kitchens will be here shortly."

"Thank ye," she said, braving a step into the passageway.

"I'm under strict orders to keep ye in the chamber. Please doona make any trouble."

"Trouble?" she arched her eyebrows, not understanding why this stranger would believe she'd cause any problems. "What has Alex told ye? Do ye have a name?"

"Craig MacKay."

"Tis good to meet ye, Craig. And yer friend?"

The other soldier frowned at Keely. "Cavas."

"Cavas?" she asked curiously. "Tis an Irish name, is it not?'

"Aye," the guard confirmed. "My mother is a MacKay, my sire, a MacMurra."

"Would ye deny a lass a bit of fresh air?"

Cavas shook his head. "Ye've had plenty of air from what I've heard, Lady Keely. Tis better to keep to yer room until the laird says otherwise." The young guard gestured for Keely to return to her bedchamber. "If ye require anything, doona hesitate to ask."

Cavas was bolder and less congenial than his cohort. Convincing him to turn a blind eye while she ran away would be near impossible. "I require use of the privy." Perhaps she could kick out the back wall and escape. Or she'd feign illness and linger in the privy for hours until the guards gave up and went for help. Anything was better than passing time alone in the bedchamber that used to be occupied by Alex's mother.

Though Keely wasn't superstitious by nature, even she could feel a presence in the room. Good or evil, she couldn't say. But there was something or someone there, and she preferred not to find out.

"The laird had the good sense to foresee such a request," Craig said. "See, milady?"

He picked something up off the floor and then offered it to Keely.

She stared at the bronze chamber pot. "Alex is a considerate man," she said severely, her hope of escape shrinking by the moment. "What about my bags?"

"Aye," Craig said. "I am to tell ye that a maid will attend to yer things as soon as possible."

"Very well." She withdrew inside the bedchamber, and Cavas gave her a triumphant look as he closed the heavy wood door. Though it hadn't been barred from the outside, Keely knew she was a prisoner, not a guest. At least in the dungeon the darkness shrouded her from the humiliation she experienced whenever a MacKay stared at her in judgement.

As for the general discomfort of the room, her gaze zig-zagged from the bed to the hearth, the padded chairs in front of it, to the dressing table in the corner, the narrow window on the far wall, to the high ceiling, where someone had lovingly painted colorful flowers and the sun. It felt strange, as if she was intruding on someone's privacy. "I doona want to be here," she whispered. "And if ye're here, whoever it be, could ye kindly tell the Lord all I wish for is freedom."

Nothing stirred, and Keely took a deep breath, relieved and surprised by the ridiculous fear inside her. Spirits were for children to believe in, not grown women, and surely not the educated daughter of a laird. She claimed one of the chairs in front of the fire, tucking her legs underneath her gown, letting the heat melt away her disappointment.

Perhaps God had put her here for a reason. To help Alex, to aid Clan MacKay. Their greatest enemy had provided food and shelter for her—asking little in return. Only that she provided companionship for her dearest friend, Helen Sutherland, and to sometimes pay special attention to Earl Sutherland's illegitimate son, Struan.

Struan remained ever respectful, but his eyes told a different story. The thought sent a chill spiraling down Keely's spine. The man had a way with words, could soothe the wildest mare, even quiet a crying child. But when Keely had been alone with him, their conversation more personal, more honest, she'd sensed the restlessness inside him, seen the resentment on his face. Struan Sutherland did not like living between two worlds.

His father, the earl, had seduced Struan's much younger mother, a visiting, distant cousin. After she died on her birthing bed, the earl had taken pity on his helpless son, claiming him—gifting him with the Sutherland name. But that rare mercy had cost Struan. As a nameless bastard, little would have been expected of him. But as a true son of the earl, though he would never inherit a title, he was expected to serve his father as loyally as his other two, legitimate sons.

It left Struan wanting more, and Keely had involuntarily become his confidant, often left for hours in the great hall listening to his secrets.

Why she was so focused on Struan she couldn't say. Only that she'd grown accustomed to his presence every day, and now that she was alone and surrounded by silence, it made her regret ever leaving Dunrobin Castle. For she truly missed Helen. And the earl had treated her as his own daughter.

But in the aftermath of the destruction of the MacKay village, the memory of the burned-out cottages, the smell of ash, and the eerie absence of people and livestock, forced her to reconsider her purpose with the Sutherlands. Just why had the laird taken her in? Why had he forbidden her from communicating with her father and clan? Why had he refused to send word to John MacKay?

The fact that she was questioning herself so critically, only lent value to Alex's suspicion. He had every reason to suspect her of spying. And the only way out of this keep was convincing him she wasn't acting on behalf of the earl.

A knock on the door startled Keely. She sprang up from the comfortable chair. "Come in."

The door opened, and a pretty, blond-haired maid came inside with a tray. "Lady Keely." She did a half curtsy, then rushed to the table, setting the tray down. "My name is Leah."

"Thank ye for the food, Leah." Keely smiled.

"Laird MacKay asked me to serve as yer maid."

"Did he?"

"Aye. Though my mother isna too pleased by it, tis my decision to make."

How would the other women treat Leah for daring to serve an outcast? "If ye change yer mind, I'd understand. I doona wish for anyone to suffer because I'm here."

Leah clicked her tongue. "Tis the older women who gossip the most."

"Aye," Keely acknowledged. "They've lived through unspeakable suffering. Today only serves as a bitter reminder of the past."

"Is it true, milady?"

Keely snorted at the girl's lack of manners, appreciating her unbridled curiosity. "What exactly are ye asking?"

"I am sorry." Leah bowed her head.

"Doona apologize, Leah. Ask what ye will."

Their gazes met, and Leah nodded. "Ye loved Alex but married Laird John?"

The girl reminded Keely so much of herself when she was but sixteen. "How old are ye, Leah?"

"Seventeen."

"So very young," Keely said.

"But ye are not much older, milady."

"Perhaps not," Keely said, "but I feel verra old today."

"Ye're tired, milady. In need of food and rest."

"It will be verra hard to sleep after everything that happened..."

"Ye mean Angus's death? Doona fash over that man," Leah said. "He had a violent nature, always quick to anger—cruel to his wife and son."

A new wave of sadness washed over Keely. "So I made a woman a widow and left her son fatherless?" Sinking onto a bench, Keely covered her face with both hands and took a shaky breath. "Is there no end to the bloodshed today?"

Keely heard the maid pour something into a cup, then she padded over to where Keely sat. "Some wine?"

Keely gazed up at her. "Thank ye."

"Tis not yer fault, milady. Mary MacKay would praise ye for freeing her of such a husband if she could. He cared nothing for his family, often leaving them hungry and cold. Because of ye, in a few months, I am sure she will marry again."

"How can ye be so sure?" Keely sipped her wine, savoring the full flavor, eager for the numbness it would bring.

"Though Mary does nothing unseemly, tis no secret she an Neil MacKay, one of Laird John's captains, are in love."

"Would Laird John have approved of the match?"

"Aye."

"Then I shall quietly consider it a blessing for Mary and her son."

"Ye're nothing like the women said," Leah observed.

"Nay?"

"Ye're kind, milady. Considerate. And beautiful."

"I'm afraid yer kinswomen would be disappointed to hear it."

The maid waved her hand in the direction of the door. "Wouldn't be the first time I've given them a reason to be unhappy with me. I care little for what they say."

For such a young lass, Leah had a good head on her shoulders. "Who is yer father?"

"Adam MacKay."

Keely's head snapped up. "*The* Adam MacKay? The famed outlaw?"

"Aye, the very one."

"Then we have something in common, Leah. We're both

outsiders."

The lass smiled. "Aye. Now can I serve ye some bread and cheese?"

"Have ye forgotten about the question ye asked earlier?"

Leah shook her head.

"Aye, it is true. I loved Alexander MacKay more than any woman had a right to."

"But ye married Laird John."

"I did. For reasons I canna share."

"I understand, milady, and willna question ye again."

Keely didn't mind the presumptuous girl, in fact, she welcomed the company. Somehow, Leah had taken her mind off her present situation, making her feel welcome—even if that pleasure was fleeting, it eased Keely's sadness.

"Ye are welcome to serve as my maid, Leah. Tell Alex I am grateful for his kindness." Though she knew it had nothing to do with goodwill, she wouldn't give Alex the satisfaction of seeing her upset. No, she must demonstrate her resolve in a way Alex would understand. Without losing control of her emotions, which meant no tears—no tenderness of any kind. She'd made that mistake already. It wouldn't happen again.

The maid brought her a plate of food and refilled her cup with wine. Surprised by how hungry she actually was, Keely ate three pieces of bread with cheese, and finished a third cup of wine before she yawned.

"If ye will allow me to help ye," Leah offered. She walked behind Keely and started to unbind her hair, running her fingers through the long strands. "After ye rest, I'll see to getting some hot water and a tub so ye can bathe before the evening meal."

"The bath is welcome, but I willna be taking food belowstairs."

"Laird Alex has ordered ye bathed and properly dressed,

milady."

"Did he now?" Keely turned around, looking at the maid. "And what else has Laird Alex demanded?"

"To immediately notify him if ye refuse, so he can carry ye to the great hall if necessary. He made it verra clear that ye enjoyed being toted around like a sack of grain."

Keely snorted, not at all humored by Alex's pomposity. If he ever tried to carry her again, Keely would ... well she'd ... damn if she knew what she'd do. Pride and honor must be retained in front of his clan. Though she'd taken the MacKay name, underneath she was an Oliphant. And her people were stubborn and strong, too. No man would make demands of her, not in the way Alex suggested.

"Tell Alex I will join him for supper when *I am ready* to do so."

Chapter Seven

"I DINNA ASK for this," Alex complained, pacing the length of his father's solar. The council had gathered in private to discuss the clan's future with him. "Why do ye think I'd want to be laird?"

"What in God's name ails ye? Tis the natural order of things. Ye are Laird John's brother—yer sire's last son."

Alex eyed the older man sitting at the head of the table, Mathe MacIver, a lifelong friend and distant kinsman from his mother's side of the family. "And what great things did my brother accomplish that ye would find it necessary to choose me as the next laird?"

Mathe rubbed his bearded chin, looking to his left and right to get answers from the other men.

"He kept the peace," one offered.

"Peace?" Alex was tempted to laugh. "Shall I recite the missive my brother sent? Relay the desperation he expressed?"

Mathe slammed his hand down on the aged wood, obviously offended by Alex's questions. "Did ye ever consider yer brother would do anything to get ye back here because he had the foresight to understand he might not survive a battle against the Sutherlands? That pleading and begging wasn't beyond him if it meant protecting the clan?"

"I guess we shall never know, my friend. John is dead, And I have a ship waiting."

"Curse those heathens," Mathe said. "Blast that damned vessel—may it crash and sink on the first wind—ye with it, if ye dare abandon us again."

Alex's hand instinctively went to the hilt of his sword. "If ye weren't a trusted kinsman…"

"What?" Mathe shot up from his chair. "Tell me."

"I'd drive my blade through yer gullet."

"Ye speak against yerself, Laird Alex."

"How?" He locked gazes with his formidable cousin.

"My words should mean nothing if ye doona have interest in this clan's future success."

"If I dinna care, old man, I wouldna be here."

"Good." Mathe reclaimed his seat. "Have the heathen ways so polluted yer Christian heart?"

Alex relaxed his stance, removing his hand from his sword. "Depends on the man asking."

Mathe arched his brows. Everyone in the room knew him to be a devout follower of God. Nothing could tempt him away from his steadfast faith, like nothing could force Alex back into it.

"What happened in the desert, Alex? Why do ye shun yer responsibilities so easily?" Jamie asked.

Nothing bad had happened. He'd welcomed the change, perhaps too eagerly, shedding his tartan like a viper shed its skin. "Stop the asking."

"Is it the lass?" Mathe pressed.

"Return her to Laird Oliphant. He'll see her punished and wed to the type of man who will lock her up so ye never have to set eyes upon her again," another council member offered.

The idea of another man touching Keely, bedding her, and filling her belly with his unborn babe made Alex angry. Though he despised the lass for what she'd done, he couldna abide the thought of her being married off to a stranger. But that's what would happen if he sent her home. No father would keep a daughter that brought shame to her family and clan. Keely had done so by seeking refuge with the Sutherlands.

His only recourse was to find a MacKay to marry her. "The lass isna going home."

"What?" Mathe asked.

"Ye heard me."

Jamie pretended to clear his ears of something. "But I dinna."

Alex met his cousin's hard stare. "Aye, ye did."

"The MacKays need an heir," Mathe said. "And though the lass is treacherous by nature, she is young and beautiful–perhaps worth keeping."

Alex's jaw clenched instantly. Just because he refused to let her go dinna mean he wanted her for himself. "I doona need ye to play matchmaker for me." He shook his head at Mathe. "In order to right the dishonor she brought on this clan, Keely must be married to a MacKay. A man up to the challenge of bedding the wench." Alex turned his attention on young Jamie. "One with plenty of experience where women are concerned. One who can guarantee Keely won't want to escape their bedchamber."

The council members chuckled, except for Jamie.

"My brother, God keep him, was not the sort to cavort with women out of wedlock. His inexperience dinna help where Keely was concerned. She's a spirited lass." *Spirited. Passionate. Beautiful. And a damned liar.*

"God bless, Laird John." Mathe crossed himself, his sadness palpable.

"Aye." Jamie crossed himself, too.

"Before I had a chance to suggest what man I thought should be the next laird, ye elected me."

"Yer dissention doesna matter, Laird Alex. Ye canna undo what has already been decided. And we've all taken the knee—pledging our allegiance to ye."

Alex's gaze slowly crept over the four men at the table. Each nodded in agreeance. Curse his misfortune. But, there was another solution, one that crossed his mind out of desperation. His family's branch of the MacKays was one of several independent clans. If the council voted to dissolve their branch and joined forces with the main clan, the Sutherlands wouldn't be so quick to attack again.

Or, as laird, he alone could make that choice. But something so underhanded would count as the ultimate betrayal. As much as he dinna want to be laird, he would never deceive his kinsmen. "There is another choice."

Mathe studied him suspiciously, and Jamie just gaped at him.

"What are ye suggesting?" Mathe queried.

"Join forces with a larger branch of the MacKays."

The room grew silent, and Alex knew the answer—they wouldn't do it.

"Yer sire would be ashamed of ye!" Mathe chastised him. "Give up our lands, our independence? For what? To become the chattel of a stranger?"

His brother had said something similar when they'd met on the beach. "I could negotiate the terms, assure that ye and the other captains retain yer positions and wealth."

"Cuimhnich air na daoine às an tàinig u." Mathe shook his head in disgust.

Alex remembered well enough who he came from and dinna need the captain to tell him so. "I am my sire's son, make no mistake, Mathe. But I am a man without roots—and in good conscience, canna claim what rightfully belongs to another."

Mathe cast his gaze downward, his expression one of deep disappointment.

Diplomacy wasn't a gift Alex possessed. He always spoke bluntly, preferring truth over softening the blow of what he had to say. "If ye willna join forces with another clan, then elect Jamie as the new laird."

"Jamie, Graham, and Dag, will ye give me time alone with Alexander?" Mathe asked.

The council members dinna need any encouragement to take their leave. One by one, they exited the solar, avoiding Alex. Once the door closed, Mathe turned to Alex.

"I dinna know what happened to ye during yer travels. Maybe ye've shed too much blood, killed too many men and fooked too many women to know the difference between right or wrong. But I will tell ye now, whether ye wish to hear it or not, if ye abandon us again, it will destroy any hope yer people have for a secure future."

Alex walked to the closest wall and rested his forehead against the rough, gray stones. "My father loved ye."

"Aye," Mathe said. "And he loved ye—more than ye know."

Alex grunted in doubt. "My sire dinna know me."

"Ye're wrong, Alex. The day he realized ye weren't coming back, it broke his heart. And John's, too."

His last claim made Alex whip around. "Doona lie to me."

"Lie?" Mathe stood up and walked around the table. "Gaze upon these ancient stones, lad. Imagine how many generations of MacKays have stood in this same chamber revealing secrets unknown to the clan. If these stones could talk, what do ye think they'd say?"

Alex ran his fingers over the wall, in awe of the men who had cut the rocks so perfectly, then fit them together to form the great keep that had provided shelter for his family for seven generations. "I doona ken."

"Clean the sand from yer ears, boy, and listen to me. See with yer heart, not yer eyes alone. Ye fear the unknown, nothing more. If ye truly wanted to go, ye would have never raised the sword in defense of our clan against the Sutherlands. And that woman—Keely Oliphant—she wouldna be here, either. Ye're afraid of what the future holds—yet willing to hold on to the past."

Alex was silent for a moment. "Ye're a fool."

"Nay. I'm a MacKay." Mathe thumped his chest. "And so are ye."

"Not by choice."

Mathe stood directly in front of him now, his eyes narrowed.

Alex's heart hammered as Mathe gripped his shoulders. "I doona know what gods ye worshipped in the heathen lands—what men ye served, but ye're here now. Called home by the Almighty. Dinna ye see that, lad?"

See what? The remnants of his father's life that was unfairly cut short? Or his brother, Laird John, also known as Gentle John? What legacy would Alex leave behind if he were laird of the MacKays? None. Because Alex wasna meant to be laird. He was a ruthless mercenary interested in one thing—gold. "I told ye before, old man, I'm a sellsword, not a bloody laird."

Mathe raised his hand and slapped Alex's cheek. Shock and rage swirled within Alex's gut. The lingering sting from Mathe's calloused hand deepened his anger. Their gazes locked, and Alex beat back the urge to retaliate. No man, not even his sire, had ever assaulted him so shamelessly.

"I am prepared to die." Mathe dropped to his knees and bowed his head, pulling the length of his gray-streaked hair to one side, revealing the back of his neck.

"Why did ye strike me?" Alex growled.

"I acted on behalf of yer da. For never has a son of the Highlands acted so wretchedly. Ye are a selfish, lad, Alexander Joseph MacKay. I'd rather die than live to see the day this clan is destroyed from the inside-out."

Alex huffed out a frustrated breath. Curse his birthright. Damn the Highlands. And to Hades with the beautiful past that sat abovestairs awaiting word on her future life. "Keep yer head, old man."

Alex pivoted, taking in the details of his father's solar—the hearth and mantle, shelves packed tight with manuscripts, the wood benches, padded chairs from Italy, the weapons hanging on the wall, and his ma's tapestries. Nothing had changed, only him. He strode to the door, forced it open, and headed out of the keep. The only cure for his rage? A heedless mount unafraid of galloping blindly across the rock-ridden terrain Alex once considered home.

Chapter Eight

"WHAT DO YE mean she willna come down for the evening meal?" Alex blinked in disbelief, wondering if Leah had misunderstood Keely. "Did ye relay my message word for word?"

"Aye, milord, I did."

"Not forgetting the part about carrying her down if I must?"

"Aye, I was sure to say so."

Alex couldna accept more disobedience. First his council, and now Keely. "Are ye laughing at me, Leah?"

"Never, Laird Alex." She gave a quick curtsey. "Lady Keely gave a firm answer. She has requested that I bring a tray to her room."

"Did she bathe?"

"Aye."

"Pick a gown from the ones I sent?"

"Aye."

"So, she is ready for supper?"

"I even dressed her hair."

"Ye're dismissed, Leah. Leave the lady's food to me." Alex stomped up the curved, narrow stairs. Keely had no right to defy him. Neither did Mathe or Jamie, or the other captains on the council, or his many cousins, warriors, tenants, servants, or any other bloody fool who drank his wine and gorged themselves from the meat set upon his table.

"And when did ye start referring to anything in this keep as yer own?" he asked himself.

Arriving at Keely's doorway, he quickly waved the two guards away. "Rest for a bit. I will watch over Lady Keely."

The men thanked him and bowed.

Once they were out of sight, Alex turned back to the arched door. His sire had commissioned a famous saor from France to craft it. A unicorn lying in a bed of grass and thistle graced the top. Clan MacKay was written in Gaelic, English, and French underneath the scenery. His ma had adored the unusual wedding gift. Alex shook his sentimental thoughts off, and banged on the polished wood. "Lady Keely."

When no answer came, he knocked again.

"Who is at my door?" Keely finally called out. She pretended not to know who stood outside her chamber.

"Alexander."

"Go away."

He clenched his teeth. How long could he endure this torture? How long was he expected to swallow his pride while his inferiors took advantage of him? Aye, he'd been gone for too long and understood it would take time for the clan to respect his authority. But this woman—this she-devil, this hellion, she wasna part of his plan. In no way had he agreed to deal with Keely.

"Open the door, Keely."

Footsteps sounded. "Ye commanded me to stay in this chamber, Alex. And that's what I intend to do."

"Ye'll come when ye're called, woman."

"Like one of yer beasts? Perhaps ye would have more success with the hounds who lie underneath yer table."

"God so help me, Keely..."

"Ye're beyond redemption, Alexander. Remember? Doona call upon the Almighty for patience."

Unable to abide her sharp tongue any longer, Alex forced his way inside, causing Keely to stumble back as he entered the chamber. "What are ye trying to hide?" he asked, gazing about the generous space. "There will be no more secrets between us, Keely."

She tilted her head back defiantly, her blue eyes blazing like the fire in the hearth. "I demand my freedom. Send me home."

"Ye *are* home. Or did ye forget those vows in the kirk? Where ye pledged yer heart and body to John. And absolute obedience to this clan."

"In name only," she shot back.

"Tis that name that binds ye to me. To this keep. To these lands. By law, ye are a MacKay. Not an Oliphant."

She swallowed hard, carefully contemplating her retort. "I am more Sutherland than MacKay. For I've lived at the earl's pleasure much longer than I ever lived by yers."

He growled as he launched himself at her. Hearing those words come out of her lovely mouth made him crazy. A slap in the face or a punch in the gut would have been less painful. He backed her into the nearest wall, then took hold of her chin. "Are ye a Sutherland whore?"

Her eyes grew wide. "Never."

"Are ye a Sutherland spy?"

"Nay."

"Are ye betrothed to one of the earl's sons?"

"How could I be? Until today, I was married to John."

"Then ye are a MacKay." He released her chin, but didn't back away. "I forbid ye from ever speaking that name in my presence. Under this roof, even. For no lady promised to a MacKay will ever claim to be connected to the Sutherlands."

She nodded in acquiescence, thinking better of challenging him again. "What did ye mean by, 'I am promised to a MacKay'?"

"The council agreed unanimously that ye must wed a MacKay in order to maintain clan honor. Ye left John, Keely, but ye'll not do it again. Whatever man is chosen, he won't be an inexperienced lad or a monk like my departed brother. He'll be a man. And ye better believe he'll demand his marital rights—even if a room full of maids have to hold ye down for it."

A garbled sound came out of her mouth as she pushed him away. "Get out!" she screamed.

"Aye," he said, almost regretting he'd caused the agony on her beautiful face. "Take the night to come to terms with yer fate, lady. Come tomorrow, after my brother is buried, we shall revisit this conversation."

KEELY WOULD PRAY fervently that Alex had the sense to see how wrong he was about everything. That he'd change his mind and send word to her father. She'd rather face her sire's wrath than spend another day inside the MacKay keep. Sadness had been heaped upon her since the moment she'd crossed their border.

Stripping off the wool gown, she laid it over the back of a nearby chair, then sat on the edge of the mattress, drawing her knees to her chest. In a fairer world, she'd have the freedom to go where she wished. But such a life dinna exist. She could only fantasize about fulfilling her girlhood dream of travelling—visiting Italy and France, perhaps to the exotic places where Alex had lived for so long—where the sun kissed the sand.

Just then, she heard a bell ring from outdoors and rushed to the single, narrow window in her room. It was wide enough to see down to the bailey where a small crowd had gathered as a man dressed in a black tunic and breeches called out the name of her departed husband as he rang the hand bell.

"Our kindly Laird John Simon Alexander MacKay was taken too soon," the man said. "On the morn, he will be laid to rest in the kirk…"

Keely backed away from the window, disliking what the mort bell represented. Evil spirits were warded off by its sound. Keely remembered the same ritual from her mother's funeral. The bell used in her ma's procession had been baptized by the priest. The bell ringer headed the long line of mourners that would walk the three miles to where her mother wished to be buried.

Returning to the bed, she crawled to the center, tired but unable to keep bittersweet memories from flooding her mind. The very night Laird John had been told Keely had accepted his offer for marriage. He requested an audience with her in the women's solar, with only an elderly, deaf maid serving as chaperone.

"Why?" he'd asked. "Ye belong to Alex."

"If ye think so," Keely countered, "then why did ye ask me to marry ye?"

John rubbed his noble chin. Unlike his brother, John's features were softer, his eyes deep set and compassionate. Aye, warmth radiated from his strong body, but not the heat of passion that affected Keely whenever she stood in front of Alex. This wouldna be a marriage built on lust or love, it would be one of respect and appreciation. She could live with that only if she dinna have to see Alex every day.

"Do ye always answer questions with questions?" he asked.

"Only if I seek my own answers."

John chuckled. "Alexander failed to claim ye. How could any man resist ye, Keely?"

As she'd been told by John's father, her future husband had no idea that his sire had arranged for Keely to marry his eldest son, not Alex. The MacKays and Oliphants wished to unite in blood—and power. They'd been at peace for generations, so it seemed the natural thing to do. Keely's sire had sent a missive, demanding her obedience and absolute silence.

Alexander is young, her father had written, he'll recover, as will ye once a bairn grows inside yer belly. Make me proud, daughter, and I'll reward ye and yer husband.

There'd been no recourse, she was an only daughter with six brothers. It would serve her family best if she married the heir to the MacKay clan, not the second son.

"May I kiss ye, Keely?" John asked. "To seal our betrothal."

Keely gazed at the old woman who had fallen asleep on the stool in the corner. "Aye," she said, appreciative of John's gentle demeanor.

Expecting him to tug her into his arms, she closed her eyes, waiting impatiently to discover if he'd heat her blood the way Alex did. Much to her disappointment, John planted a kiss on her forehead first. And after she opened her eyes, staring up at him in complete disappointment, he gave her a chaste kiss on the lips.

"I look forward to our future life, Lady Keely." He bowed, then left the solar.

Keely didn't move for a long time. She touched her lips, regretful that nothing had sparked between them. John's touch dinna awaken any feelings inside her, dinna raise gooseflesh on her arms. Tears formed in her eyes, but she quickly palmed them away. Feelings dinna matter. Keely would do her duty, solidify the alliance between her family and the MacKays, and hopefully, provide an heir. She'd focus on that to help get her through the hard times she knew she'd face concerning Alex. She loved him, completely. Wanted him. It would take time to forget him…

Keely returned to the present.

In five long years she hadn't forgotten Alex. Not one night had passed without him invading her thoughts or dreams. Some of those dreams were disturbingly real and involved rigorous lovemaking, though she'd never seen Alexander naked, or ever been naked with him. Her fertile imagination made up for her lack of carnal knowledge of her beloved, for she could envision every inch of his muscle-graced body, the spark in his green eyes, even feel his strong fingertips tracing the contours of her own form.

Like most women, she craved passion. And there was no lack of talk from the married women or wanton maids that served in the Sutherland household. They described bedsport with as much enthusiasm as any man. But with Alex, she dinna need all the wooing—just him.

"Just him," she repeated out loud.

What was wrong with her? Alex dinna like her—in fact, if she knew anything about the man she once loved, he might even hate her, which was hard to accept. "Tomorrow," she whispered, "while the funeral is going on, I will leave this place—forever."

Chapter Nine

ONCE THE LAST warrior left the kirk, Alex sat down on one of the rough-hewn benches in the back. He'd suffered through the funeral mass, neither embracing or rejecting the words the priest had spoken in honor of his brother. Faith in anything but himself exposed Alex to weakness, and made it necessary for him to live within the boundaries of the church and law. He preferred owing allegiance to no one. It would make it easier to leave this place.

"Laird Alex," Father Michael approached.

"I wish ye wouldna call me laird."

"Why?" the priest asked. "Tis yer rightful title."

Alex shook his head. "Mathe..." he said sourly. "The old man has been nipping at yer ear."

The priest cleared his throat. "Captain Mathe spoke with me."

"Aye. And I will tell ye the same thing I told him and the council. I have no desire to..."

"Yer soul is in jeopardy, milord. I am aware of yer many sins—murder—blasphemy, fornication—even greed."

Alex chuckled at the last one. "Every Highlander is guilty of greed, Priest. Even the Pope is guilty of greed."

Father Michael wobbled a bit, quickly seating himself on the bench. "Ye'd accuse the Holy Father of such a vice?"

"I'd accuse any man of wanting silver and gold, lands, and power. Tis inherent in every man born."

"Christ was *born*."

"Doona try to trap me by using my own words against me, Father Michael. Speak yer piece, then leave me to contemplate my own future."

"The clan needs ye. The church…"

"Needs the annual donation my sire and brother generously sent to Rome?" Alex reached inside his tunic, pulling out a small leather pouch. "I willna deny ye what funds ye've honestly earned, Father. I'll deny no man his living. Will ye?" He offered the priest the money.

Reluctantly, Father Michael accepted the pouch, placing it on the space between them. "Nay. God commanded every good man to toil."

Alex scrubbed his face. "Tis good to know the Lord willna deny me a living either."

"Alexander. I've known ye since ye were a bairn. Ye were a God-fearing lad, curious and of strong moral character. If yer sire ordered ye to do something, without hesitation ye'd do it. I remember the boy who sat quietly upon his bench, listening contentedly to the liturgy, asking for guidance if ye dinna understand something. What happened to that lad?"

He stared at the priest. "I grew up."

"Will ye listen to reason, Alex? Remember the story about the man who built his home on sand?"

"Aye. Ye couldna pick a better illustration, Father. My home *is* built on sand, and I intend to travel there within a sennight." Through with the priest, Alex stood. "I've chosen Jamie as the next laird."

Father Michael nodded in appreciation. "He's capable."

"Aye."

"But his proclivity for women…"

"Will be over the moment he weds Keely Oliphant."

"What?"

"A goodly match, I think. It will finally achieve what my sire long wished for, a true alliance between the MacKays and the Oliphants. United, we will have access to more soldiers and coin to defend ourselves against the Sutherlands."

"Ye'd speak of such things when yer only brother has been freshly entombed within these sacred walls."

"Life goes on, Father, does it not? John died for the very reason I wish to hurry my cousin's nuptials with the lass. I will make sure the clan is secure and well-funded before I sail for Constantinople. And in the future, rest assured I will continue to send coin to maintain this place. I willna leave my kinsmen hungry and vulnerable."

"Though I believe ye, time and distance have a way of making a man forget his responsibilities." The priest arched a brow.

Alex chose to say nothing as he left the kirk. Now he could add the priest to his list of disobedient servants. When his sire had been laird, fear kept his subordinates in line. The problem here now was none of these people really knew Alex or what he was capable of, even though he'd killed a man yesterday in defense of Keely.

HE WANDERED INSIDE the great hall, ignoring the invitations to have a drink in appreciation of his brother. Food and ale were plentiful today, for the MacKays dinna just mourn a lost laird, they celebrated their accomplishments with a feast and music, even dancing once everyone was drunk enough.

Alex wanted nothing to do with it. Just as he'd told the

priest, his clan needed to see that life would go on without Laird John, and now, without him. He sought refuge in the solar, happy to keep company with Petro. More intelligent than any man he'd ever met, the Italian had a peculiar way of calming Alex's inner storms.

"I am truly sorry for your loss." The scholar looked up from a manuscript.

"Thank ye for attending the funeral."

"Any family of yours..."

"Is not a bloody friend," Alex interrupted him.

"The weight of the world is upon your shoulders?"

"I wish it were so easily explained."

"Share the burden, then."

"Ye couldna possibly understand," Alex said.

"What exactly?"

"The complications of a Highland clan."

Petro's laughter filled the chamber. "Are you certain, my friend? I have three hundred and sixty-two cousins in Rome alone. Royal blood and the blood of traitors runs through my veins. My father outlived four wives, sired eighteen children, and calls himself king when he's at home, though he's a mere lord. And you claim I wouldn't understand your life?"

Alex grabbed a cup off the table and drank down the remaining ale in it. "I stand corrected, then. Did ye say eighteen children?" The very idea of siring so many bairns made his balls ache, and not in a good way. "How did he..."

"I believe it involved food and wine, and lots of fucking."

Alex snorted. "Are all of yer people so vigorous?"

A spark of mischievousness lighted Petro's dark eyes. "Give me permission to mingle with your maids, and I will get an answer for your question."

"Nay," Alex said. "We sail soon, and I'll not have ye get a

poor lass with child."

"Why would you leave this place?" His friend's expression sobered. "If I never feel the oppressive heat of the east again, I will be a happy man."

"Ye wish to go home?"

"I wish to serve you, *here*."

"Where?"

"Scotland."

"My days are numbered here, my friend. But if ye wish to stay, I am sure my cousin would be grateful to gain a capable adviser."

"You'd recommend me?"

"I'll write ye a letter of recommendation now. One ye can take wherever ye go. But I must tell ye, a man of yer talents could find work in the king's court. Ye'd be well compensated, maybe even gain a title in time."

"I'm the youngest child from a second wife, Alex. Wealth and titles mean little to me. Only my elder brothers received lands and money. There wasn't enough to go around. My father kindly financed my education, then told me to make my own way in the world. Though I could return to Italy and find a wife and buy an estate of my own with the gold I've earned, I would get bored—and surely stray from my marriage bed. The daughters of Italy are too angelic for me."

"It seems Constantinople has ruined our chances at happiness." In that part of the world, people existed without pretense. Everyone knew their purpose, their place. There was no shame in a man earning coin for killing or paying to enjoy the bed of a beautiful woman. In Scotland, such actions demanded explanation, penance, and sometimes death.

"No," Petro disagreed. "You deprive yourself of joy."

"What do ye mean?" He eyed the Italian. Everyone else had

pecked at Alex, why shouldn't his most devoted friend take a turn?

"If God wished you to go back to Constantinople, then I am sure we'd be on the ship already. Every day you spend here, my friend, you get a little more entrenched in the politics at home."

"I've offered a logical solution."

"On *your* terms."

"There are no other terms."

"The council serves in absence of a leader, does it not?"

"Aye."

"And you are an unwilling laird."

"A proxy laird," Alex corrected.

"But still laird."

"Yer point?"

"When a man comes into power, whether he wishes it or not, he must examine his conscience, determine what keeps him from his true destiny."

"Ye know my reasons."

"I do."

"Is that not good enough?"

Petro averted his eyes. "I think not."

"How so?"

Petro turned back to him. "How many people have told you the answer already?'

"It doesna matter what anyone else says. I asked ye."

The scholar closed the leather-bound manuscript, then stood. "I prefer to answer while standing in front of you."

"So I can punch ye if yer words offend?"

Petro chuckled. "A risk I'm willing to take."

Though short, the Italian was muscular and confident. And when necessary, he could swing a sword. Alex waited for him to speak, though he could guess what would be said.

"The woman," Petro started. "She belongs to you. Not your cousin. Not her father. Not any other man."

Alex rolled his eyes and crossed his arms. "Keely."

"Lady Keely," Petro repeated. "You have the *only* claim on her. I've read your sire's journals, and your brother's. Both acknowledged your right to her. Furthermore, you exchanged consents, which in the eyes of the law, means you are already married to the woman."

"This canna be true. We never…"

"But the promise was made. Was it not?"

"Aye—more than once. In every way possible without having carnal knowledge of her." Memories burned bright and passionate in Alex's mind now. The feel of Keely's plush lips on his, the soft curves of her body, the way she squirmed and bucked underneath him when he nearly claimed her maidenhead—before reason took over. He'd wanted to marry her in the eyes of God before he made love to her. Honor demanded it. But his body disagreed on every level—burning for the dark-haired beauty still.

"Unfortunately, Alex, it is the truth. Your brother's marriage to Lady Keely was illegitimate. You are her husband."

"Annulment."

Petro shook his head. "The very thing you denied her. In order to keep peace with her clan, and to protect your people and assets, you must marry her again, only this time, do it with witnesses. Otherwise, according to the law, she must be returned to her family."

"I have thought this over—considered every possible argument."

"Except the finer details of the law. Even canon law."

How could Alex disagree with a scholar from Rome, the very place the pope lived? Petro had a strong mind, greater than his own. Alex raked his fingers through his hair. What of his desert stronghold? His soldiers? Concubines? Servants? His freedom? Surely this news dinna change anything. If Petro dinna share the information with anyone…

"What will ye do with this knowledge?"

"Tell the truth," Petro said in a subdued voice.

"To who?'

"The council has requested a meeting with me."

What right did his captains have to speak with Petro? "Why?"

"On the occasions I was present while you were debating with the council and stormed off, a couple of the members questioned me. I am many things, Alexander, but not a liar. Not if your life doesn't hang in the balance."

"Ye'd lie to save my life?"

Petro nodded.

"Then lie for me now."

"No."

"This is such a moment."

"*Am fear nach misnich, cha bhuannaich.*"

The familiar words made Alex freeze. His body began to quake with emotion. "Where did ye steal those words?"

"From letters I discovered in your father's belongings. Letters to you. You know this saying?"

"The man who dares not, wins not," Alex said. "Something my da often whispered to me as a boy when I feared anything."

"And do you fear something now?" Petro pressed.

"I find peace among the heathens," Alex said.

"There are no unbelievers here except for you."

"I believe…"

"In what?"

"Myself."

"Is that enough, Alexander?'

He dinna know at this point. Thinking hurt too much right now. And there were letters, from his beloved father. Why hadn't his brother told him right away? Sent them to him? Because John probably believed he dinna deserve such a rare gift. "Give me the letters."

Petro walked back to the table, picked up a pile of missives tied together with a leather chord, then offered them to Alex. "May God open your eyes, Alex."

He hugged the missives to his chest. "Dinna look for me, Petro. And tell anyone else who wishes to disturb me that I will punish them severely for such an offense."

Petro bowed, unable to hide the smile on his face.

Alex ignored him. There were more important matters to tend to now. First the missives, then his wife. The idea of having a wife dinna bother Alex overmuch, only the fact of who that wife was—Keely Oliphant—the bane of his very existence in the Highlands.

Chapter Ten

KEELY HAD SPENT the better part of two days in her chamber, avoiding Alex and everyone else in Clan MacKay. If she overheard another insult or caught another maid giving her a dirty look, she'd eventually snap and defend herself. It would only deepen the rift between her and Alex. His advice? Give people time to get used to her presence.

She dinna have time to spare. Home called to her more than it ever had. To be honest, she missed her da and brothers, the games they'd play with her, and perhaps most of all, the hugs and kisses her sire freely gave. Tears filled her eyes and she let them fall. It had been a long time since she'd cried, purging the regret and sorrow she carried around. Another trait she'd gotten from her father, to keep all the pain inside. Eventually it would go away. But after five years of silence, Keely doubted it very much.

Coming back to the MacKays had proven that theory wrong. Seeing Alex, finding John dead, and almost getting killed—it sucked the strength from her body. She sagged to the floor, the deep sobs wracking her body.

"Dearest Father," she cried. "I desperately wish ye were here…"

A knock sounded and Keely dinna know what to do. There was no way to hide her grief. She forced herself to her feet, wiped the tears from her eyes and cheeks, then took a deep breath. Maybe if she dinna answer, whoever it was would go away.

Another light rap came, and she sighed.

"Who is it?"

The door opened and Jamie stuck his head inside. "Ye are summoned."

"By who?" Keely stared at Alex's handsome cousin. "I am quite comfortable in this chamber."

Jamie entered the chamber, sure to leave the door open. He took a closer look at her. "Has something happened?"

"Nay," she said. "I-I doona know how to explain it."

"Ye're scared of what's to come, lass? Miss yer family?"

It embarrassed her to admit it, but Jamie seemed genuinely concerned. "I never should have come back."

"Regrets canna fix anything, Keely. It will only make ye suffer. Alex is a reasonable man about most things."

Most things... "Not with me." Alex's cold and ugly smile when he ordered her locked in a cell had stuck in her mind like a bad dream.

"The two of ye must come to terms, lass."

She wanted nothing else but doubted it would ever happen. "Do ye know what he wants to see me about?"

Jamie shook his head. "He's been unusually quiet."

When they were younger, if Alex had something on his mind, he'd disappear. Normally, she'd await his return. But on one occasion, she sought him out. The memory of his warning echoed around her. *"Leave before ye discover the man I truly am."*

She heeded his words. What he meant exactly, she cared not to find out. The ominous look on his face had been enough.

And now, she imagined Alex the same way.

"I prefer to stay here," she said.

"I understand. But I must take ye to him," there was determination in his voice.

"Ye have forgiven him, completely?"

"Should I not?"

"We are flawed creatures," she responded. "Forgiveness doesna come easily to a Highlander, but holding a grudge does."

"He is my kinsman."

"Aye. Laird John was his brother and couldna forgive him for leaving."

"And now ye fear Alex willna forgive ye for doing the same?"

"Can ye blame me? Look what he has done to me already, Jamie. For the sake of the happy memories we share, please let me go. Turn yer back and I will slip away."

"Holy mother of Christ."

"I've offended ye?"

"Ye put me in an awkward position, lass. Isna my sympathy enough? Now ye ask me to deceive my laird?"

"I am desperate and very much alone here. What purpose could he possibly have for keeping me?"

"Ye are not alone. I am here, and there are others who understand why ye abandoned John. Some who respect yer fidelity to Alex over yer duty to yer sire."

"Then why havena they made themselves known?"

"And risk losing their place in Clan MacKay? Come now, lass. Ye know better."

"We were friends, Jamie."

"Aye. As far as I am concerned, we still are."

"May I ask a favor?"

"If it is within my power to give."

Keely walked to the table and poured herself a cup of water. She took a sip, then offered Jamie a drink. He refused. "Make up an excuse for why I canna see Alex."

He frowned at her request. "Nay."

"Please."

"Begging for the impossible is below ye, Keely. Ye're a brave lass. Face him with courage and speak yer mind. He respects honesty more than cunning."

She snorted. "Alex doesna wish me to think, only to obey."

Understanding flashed in his eyes. "Coming home has reopened his old wounds. Show him that a future here is better than going back to Constantinople."

"From what I hear, the council has tried over and over again and failed. Maybe he belongs there."

Jamie immediately straightened. "Never say that again."

"But he left. At least I stayed in the Highlands."

"If ye consider Dunrobin Castle part of Scotland. Many believe it belongs to England."

She threw her hands up in frustration. "I yield."

"Then grab yer cloak and let us go to Laird Alex."

Keely wrapped the length of brown wool around her shoulders. What did Alex want? They'd made their opinions of each other clear, and their intentions. She followed Jamie belowstairs, through the great hall where the few men and servants gathered stared at her in revilement but dinna utter a sound, then outside and through the bailey.

"Where is he," Keely asked.

"He's waiting at the loch."

"Is that where the laird conducts clan affairs now?"

Jamie stopped. "If ye wish to soothe Alex, keep yer biting remarks to yerself. Remember, ye're a constant reminder of the past, a past we want him to forget."

"Perhaps it would have been better if Angus killed me."

"Nay. Alex saved ye for a reason."

Aye, which only confused Keely, because she was sure Alex wanted her dead and gone.

They arrived at the loch, finding Alex sitting close to the water's edge, his back to them.

"Thank ye for bringing her, Jamie."

"Aye. Do ye want me to stay close?"

"Nay."

"All right." Jamie gestured for her to move closer to Alex.

She did, standing quietly beside him.

"This place holds so many memories," Alex observed.

"Happy ones?" she asked.

He turned and looked at her. "I learned to swim here. Caught my first fish here. Kissed my first lass here. Found my first love here."

His dark gaze lingered on her, and Keely knew exactly who he was talking about—her. "I remember," she whispered.

"What happened to us?" he asked.

"Fate had different plans."

"Fate is nothing. Men control their own destinies."

"And women's," she added sourly.

"Keely..." He started to get up.

"Nay." She backed away, too afraid to let him touch her, too scared to touch him.

He stayed seated. "One word from ye would have prevented yer marriage to John."

"At what cost, Alex?"

"Everything, if it meant we stayed together. Remember our promise?"

"Which one? We made so many."

"Aye," he agreed sadly. "They turned out to be empty promises."

"Again, I tell ye, we were young and foolish. Innocent."

He smiled wickedly. "There was nothing innocent about ye, lass."

"Is that what ye really think of me?"

He rubbed his chin. "I try not to think of ye anymore, Keely."

"How many insults will ye sling at me?"

"As many as it takes to rid my soul of ye," he said.

His comeback ripped a gaping hole in her chest. Those were the words of a man in love—a man who had been shattered and never found a way to put himself back together again.

"Let me go, Alex. Tis a fair solution. Ye'll be happier. Yer people will be grateful. And Lord knows, I may find my own bit of joy once I return home."

He held up his hand. "Stop."

"But..."

He shook his head and moved his attention to the water. "My father isna buried in the kirk."

Why speak of his sire now? Out of respect for the man she knew and loved, she decided to indulge Alex. "Why not?"

"The northern clans embrace their Viking roots. It is easy for a warrior to gaze across the sea and imagine his kinsmen sailing here on a longship in ancient times."

"Aye," she said. "My father did the same. The tall tales he told at feasts about the Northmen, their brutality and fearlessness, filled by childhood dreams. How many cups of ale have been raised to honor one of England's worst enemies?"

"Enough to inspire my sire to demand a burial like one of those bloody Northmen."

She looked at Alex in shock. "What do ye mean?"

"His body was washed and dressed and then placed on a ceremonial boat strewn with heather and bells. His shield and sword were placed within his cold grip, bowls of incense lit and set about him. Then the women cried the *coronach*, recalling his greatest battles as his captains pushed the boat to sea. Upon Mathe's signal, a lone archer shot a fiery arrow at the vessel, setting it afire. Twas a warrior's burial, Keely, but not a Christian one. And Father Michael canna tell me if he's in Heaven or Hades."

"Dear God..."

He continued with his story. "Mathe described the ceremony to me, but I couldna believe my sire would stray from tradition. He believed in God, but after reading his missives..." Alex showed her a stack of letters. "I'm not sure which god he worshipped."

Her heart bled for him, for no one wanted their father's soul to be lost. "His service to yer clan, his benevolence, and unwavering belief in justice have saved him. God has many names and forms, does he not? Ye've learned that on yer adventures."

Alex scratched his head. "And where did ye gain such wisdom, lass?"

"Years spent in the Sutherland library reading every manuscript I could get my hands on."

He frowned at the mention of his enemy's name, but his expression returned to normal quickly. "I doona know why I shared this story with ye. My father admired ye, Keely, even loved ye as a daughter, I think. He mentions ye many times in his letters."

"I miss yer father, Alex. Perhaps we wouldna be here if he was still laird."

"But he isna."

"Nay, he isna," she agreed. Is this what he wanted to see her about? To reminisce about things that would never be? For a brief moment she wanted to touch his face, to offer comfort, because she could see the pain in his eyes, the regret etched on his handsome face. "Where did the missives come from?"

"My secretary found them among my father's things. When I left for Constantinople, the ship I sailed on stopped in Rome first. I spent months there and met Petro de' Medici. I hired him as an interpreter. We've been together ever since."

"A valued friend?"

"More like a brother."

"I am happy ye found such a companion."

Alex nodded. "And have ye found such an ally?"

"Only one."

"A man?" His eyes narrowed.

"Nay."

"Then who?"

"I'd rather not say."

"There will be no retaliation if ye give an answer I doona like."

"Helen Sutherland."

Alex closed his eyes and drew in a stiff breath. "I know nothing about the woman."

"She isna like her brothers."

"And how well do ye know her brothers?"

"That is an unfair question."

"Is it, lass?" He placed the missives on the boulder, then started pacing. "Do ye have something to hide?"

"Nay. It's just … why do ye want to know?"

"Everything about yer past, especially the time ye spent with the Sutherlands, is of great interest to me, to my clan."

"I thought ye were leaving."

"Until this afternoon, I thought the same. But important details have come to light."

"What kind of details?"

"The kind that make a man rethink his choices."

"I'm not a Sutherland spy."

"I believe ye."

He did? "Why?"

"Ye're not stupid, Keely. So, I must accept yer explanation as to why ye showed up here when ye did. A mere coincidence, or God's hand played a part in it. Either way, I believe we were meant to see each other again."

"Thank ye for that bit of trust."

"Doona take advantage of it. If I find out ye're lying, I'll have yer heart."

The threat dinna affect her the way it should. Instead, she relied on that courage Jamie told her to find within herself. "The way I took yers?"

He gave her a scathing look—the kind she imagined he showed his fiercest enemy before he drove his sword through their gut. "Doona tempt me, lass."

She dinna understand his desires, or why he acted the way he did. "I willna grovel at yer feet, Alex."

"Why did ye leave?" he finally asked.

Should she tell him? Would he hate her that much more once she explained it? "I wasna thinking clearly when I ran away on my wedding night, Alex. John was a good man, a kind one. I-I..." The words were all jumbled up inside her head. "The thought of another man touching me..." She covered her mouth, even that partial confession would make Alex think she never stopped loving him. "It wasna what I wanted."

"Nay?" He stared at her long and hard. "What did ye want, Lady Keely?"

"The right to choose my own husband."

"And who took that freedom away from ye?"

Keely cast her gaze downward, kicking at the ground—

anything to keep from looking directly at Alex. "Circumstance."

Alex snorted. "Circumstance?"

"Aye," she said. "The kind beyond a daughter's control."

"My father and brother are gone, yer oath of secrecy died with them, Keely."

Tears filled her eyes, but she refused to give Alex the satisfaction of seeing her cry. "A promise once made must be kept, always."

Alex stepped closer, tipping her chin upward. She couldna keep from staring at him, from catching a fleeting glimpse of the compassionate man he used to be.

"I am laird now," he reminded her. "I release ye from that oath."

"I willna betray that sacred trust."

"What sacred trust? The one my sire and yer father unfairly made an inexperienced lass swear to through intimidation?"

Her heart skipped several beats. "Ye know about it?"

"My father carried a great deal of guilt after ye wed John. His missives are quite detailed. I doona think he ever intended for me to read them. Not the ones pertaining to John's life, and yer marriage."

"If ye know the truth, why are ye forcing me to say it?"

"Because I want to hear yer words."

Keely dinna like reliving the past, but everywhere she looked forced her to remember, to rethink her choices, to face her greatest sins. She'd lost five years with the people she loved, including her father and brothers. It made her heart hurt. She walked to the edge of the loch, scooped a handful of rocks from the dirt, and threw several. Ripples formed in the tranquil water. Even the winds were quiet today.

"Marrying a second son dinna appeal to my father."

"Did it please ye?"

She refused to answer.

"Keely?"

"My feelings dinna matter then, and surely doona matter now."

"I'll have an answer."

"I did as I was told."

"Until ye faced the marriage bed."

She whirled around. "Did ye bring me here to humiliate me or find a solution for our problem? John is buried. Ye're the new laird. And everything can be settled if ye just send me home where I belong. Let my da deal with my bad choices, Alex, not ye, not Clan MacKay."

Once again, Alex came to her, framing her face with his hands. His eyes were void of tenderness but not purpose. "Sending ye home would be a sign of my failure. It isna possible."

She dinna step out of reach, but stood there blinking, wondering why. Had the council demanded she be held prisoner? That Alex punish her? "Why?"

"There's consequences for everything we say and do, no?"

"Aye," she answered shakily.

"Do ye remember our last encounter here at the loch?"

She could never forget it. Never. That memory had burned a fresh path from her aching heart to her troubled mind over and over again. Especially since the day she crossed into MacKay territory and discovered the burned village. How she wished to go back and rethink her decision to flee Dunrobin Castle. "Aye."

Alex caressed her cheek with his thumb. "We pledged our hearts and souls to one another."

"We were young."

"We were in love," he said.

No. Lust. Passion. Desperate need. Hunger. Anything but

love. Seeing him in the sunlight, with his bright, green eyes focused on her, that chiseled jawline, straight nose, his shoulder-length hair, and muscular form—the way his tunic hugged his body, the way his tartan clung to his hips, revealing powerful thighs … that's what muddled her mind five years ago on a warm summer night. She could see it clearly, smell fresh heather, feel the soft grass underneath her, remember Alex's warm touch on her face and breasts, the way he pulled her gown up her legs, then parted her thighs with his knee…

"Let me show ye how much I care, lass, how much I love ye." He'd whispered those words so tenderly. "I give ye my heart, my body, and soul, Keely Oliphant. Do ye promise to be mine, to honor me with yer life, by being my wife?"

And she'd uttered *aye*, her mind and body filled with everything Alex. It had been a mistake – at least she thought so now. "Love and desire are often mistaken for the same thing," she said.

He chuckled, and she thrust her hands on her hips.

"How do ye know the difference, lass? What other man has brought ye to the edge of pleasure like me?"

She shrugged him off, but Alex wouldna relent, he grabbed her arm again. "Well?"

"Do ye think ye're the only man to offer me his love and name?"

She'd grown to hate his arrogance since she'd been back. But underneath it all, she still saw slivers of vulnerability. A man who had lost too much.

"Have ye given yerself to another, woman?"

"That is a private matter."

"I disagree," he growled.

"Ye wouldna believe me either way. If ye must know, have one of the midwives examine me."

"A suggestion I will seriously consider." He released her.

She'd like to see one of the MacKay midwives try and get her to lie down on a bed and lift her skirts. Did Alex really believe she'd shame herself by having sex out of wedlock? Honor meant everything to her, as it did Alex. Why were men judged by their character and women judged solely by their virginity?

"I'd like to return to my room."

"And I want ye to stay."

She gave up and found a patch of grass to sit on and started to hum her favorite song.

"What tune is that, lass?"

She glared at him. How could his mood change so easily? Had he lost his mind? "I doona remember the words," she lied, "just the melody."

In truth, the song spoke of two young lovers who were doomed to marry other people.

...Her golden eyes are upon me no more.
Her golden hair no longer feels like silk in my calloused hands.
Her sweet lips no longer utter my name, but the name of the man her father sold her to.
A husband who no deserves her.
A man who I would kill.
But I ken, I am in her heart—which is worth all the silver and gold in Scotland.
Worth the blood of my own Highland heart.
Her memory alone will carry me into the next life,
Where I'll stand before the Almighty and ask of him what I know he'll ask of me.
Give a reckoning of the man ye were and will be.
And I'll say of my golden eyed lass—I am no a man without her—why did ye take her from me?

And if the Almighty doesna have an answer, I'll no have one for Him...

It had stayed with her since the night of her wedding.

"I am uncivilized," he admitted as he stooped in front of her. "Prone to rage and jealousy. The idea of another man touching ye, kissing ye..." He dinna finish the thought, but slanted his mouth over hers, testing her willingness to kiss him back.

At first, it dinna feel right. Alex had no right to touch her. But something burst inside her, a need she'd long denied. One kiss from Alex awakened it again, extracting it from the depths of her heart. She twisted her fingers in his hair, pulling him close. His scent and taste overwhelmed her senses. Could this be the turning point for them? Could their bodies provide the peace she sought between them?

He broke the kiss. "Ye still want me, lass."

Damn him to the darkest depths of Hades. She'd like to slap that self-assured grin off his face.

She rejected his claim in the harshest way. "I willna turn down a kiss from a handsome man."

He offered her a mirthless laugh before he fingered a strand of her hair. "I always loved the color of yer hair, lass. Black as night, the color of sin."

She slapped his hand away. "Am I a sin, Alex?"

"Ye're a sinner, that much I know."

She stood up and brushed the grass from her backside, only too happy to leave him alone. "With yer permission..." She dipped into a curtsey. "I'd like to go inside."

Something dangerous flickered in his eyes as he straightened. "Do ye know what I do with headstrong women?"

"Alex..."

Keely turned and found Jamie standing a few feet away. The man had saved her from further humiliation.

"I asked ye to leave us alone," Alex seethed.

"The council," Jamie said. "They wish to speak to ye, *now*."

"*Magairlean*!" he cursed.

"I am sorry," Jamie offered.

"I will go, but stay with Keely. She may take the air or return to her chamber."

"I am glad our conversation is over," she called after him, unable to resist the chance to needle him once more.

He spun around. "Which part, lass? When ye misconstrued love for lust?"

She could feel her face flush. Why did he have to repeat such intimate details in front of his cousin?

"There is only one thing ye need to know, Keely. At nightfall, ye are to be delivered to the great hall where a marriage ceremony will take place."

Her heart thundered. "Who is getting married?"

Alex raised his eyebrows. "Do ye need to ask?"

"Tis my right to know if I'm expected to attend."

Alex eyed Jamie, then looked back at her. "Ye're the bride, Keely."

Frustration and confusion collided inside her, and she stumbled as if something heavy had struck her in the chest. The air around her grew thick. When he had threatened her with marriage, she thought it a ruse. "Why?" He couldna do it. "Ye will not force me to wed anyone. I want to go home."

"Look around ye, lass. This *is* home. Not Dunrobin Castle, and surely not yer sire's house. Ye're a MacKay, and by God, ye'll die one."

Her body shook uncontrollably, and then her legs gave out. "Nay," she managed to squeak before everything went black.

Chapter Eleven

ALEX CAUGHT KEELY before she hit the ground. He carried her to the rocks and sat down, balancing her on his lap. "Foolish lass," he said gently, smoothing stray hairs back from her face.

"Why do ye toy with her?" Jamie asked, looking far more concerned about Keely than Alex felt. "Ye dinna tell her the whole truth?"

"I was about to, before ye showed up."

"Ye kissed her."

"Why were ye lurking in the shadows?" His question came hard and quick.

"I dinna want to disturb ye."

"Well, ye did." Alex said, gazing at Keely's motionless form. "The she-devil ran out of strength finally."

"Keely isna what ye claim her to be, Cousin."

"If I require yer opinion on the matter, I'll ask for it."

"I'll speak freely with ye, Alex, or not at all. Is it worth all the trouble? Torturing the lass, yerself?"

"I dinna start this," Alex spat. "She did. John did."

"And Laird John paid dearly for his part. He's dead and buried. Will ye sacrifice the woman ye love to satisfy yer sick need for revenge?"

Alex burned to settle the argument with fists not words. But

Keely ... he couldna put her down. "Enough!" He dinna love Keely. That much he knew. But he did feel something for her...

Jamie held his hands up in mock surrender. "As ye command, *milord*." His cousin's words were thick with sarcasm.

"Tread carefully in the future, Jamie. Now why are ye here?"

"The council is waiting for ye."

Another opportunity for Mathe to preach to him about his lack of morals, or for Father Michael to advise him on how to save his soul? Alex had done his penance by accepting the lairdship. The council existed at his pleasure. A tradition generations of MacKay lairds had honored. The people deserved representation, and if anyone had a concern, they could reach out to a council member who, in turn, would present the issue to Alex. But if they continued to abuse their power, Alex would dissolve the council.

"Ye should take her inside," Jamie said.

Alex nodded and tapped her cheek. "Keely? Can ye hear me, lass?" She dinna move. "Keely?"

"Let me take her," Jamie offered.

"Wait." Alex gave her a gentle shake, but there was no response. "When did she have her last meal?"

"I doona know exactly."

In truth, Alex never meant for this to happen, to shock her into submission aye, but never to physically harm her. For a brief moment, he felt unbelievably close to her, as if the last five years of bitterness had melted away and the old Keely he loved and trusted was there. "She's exhausted and hungry. Take her abovestairs and stay there. I'll send Leah with food and some water. She's had an emotional shock."

Jamie collected her, cradling her in his arms. "She's yer wife, Alex. When will ye treat her as such?"

"There will be no mistaking what she is to me once we consummate this marriage. I canna change the law, Jamie. But I willna pretend to love the woman who betrayed me and dishonored the clan by abandoning John on their wedding night." How many times did he need to repeat himself? Everything he did was justified. Keely would learn the hard way. She would pay for her misdeeds.

"Did ye ever think Keely felt something in her heart, that deep inside she knew it wouldna be right to bed yer brother?"

"How could she? I dinna know anything about the law until Petro told me."

"Not direct knowledge, ye dolt."

"Would it change anything?"

"If I were in yer position, aye. The lass did what her sire commanded, what yer father made her do. She's innocent. A political pawn in a long history of alliances made through arranged marriage."

Alex rejected his explanation. "I recognize my father's role, Jamie. But her guilt is of a different nature. We were promised to each other. And instead of trusting me, she sent me away. Do ye know how many years I've suffered wondering about what happened? Why the lass rejected me?"

"So ye finally admit that ye love her."

"*Loved,*" Alex emphasized.

"That's shite," Jamie challenged him, again.

Alex growled with disapproval. "Watch yer tone, cousin."

Alex secretly envied a man like his cousin. Jamie's father was Alex's uncle. Aye, he was the next in line for the lairdship, but he'd grown up without the pressure of being a laird's son. "My relationship isna yer concern. Keeping Keely safe is."

"Just yesterday ye demanded I marry the lass. I pity the girl. For she doesna know what man will be waiting for her in the great hall. I am sure once she finds out, yer marriage bed willna be as pleasurable as ye think. Ye're a fool to take advantage of her."

"Take her away," Alex dismissed him.

Jamie did as he was told, leaving Alex alone.

Curse it all. Alex dinna like feeling trapped. But he was. And no matter how appealing that trap was, he still wished to be on his ship. Happiness would be reserved for their bedchamber, found only in their mutual pleasure.

His father and mother had shared a loving relationship, but after birthing two children, his da sought comfort elsewhere. Alex would have none of it. He'd ride his beautiful wife every night until she admitted she still loved him.

And once she was with child, he'd return to Constantinople. Fate had him by the bollocks, but he'd fight back. He tucked the treasured missives in his tunic and walked back to the keep.

Once seated at the high table with the council, Alex eyed Petro with curiosity. What had the scholar revealed to his captains?

"Thank ye for coming, Alex," Mathe said. "We are encouraged by what Petro has told us."

"And what is that?" Alex asked.

"Ye're already wed to Keely Oliphant. No man can undo what the Almighty has sanctioned."

Alex chuckled. "What if I disagree?"

Mathe shot him a look of disgust and crossed himself. "Do ye accept the laird's chair? Will ye lead Clan MacKay with honor? Provide protection, administer justice, and walk in faith with God? Give us an heir?"

Alex looked from one captain to another. All good men, all trusted advisers to his father. Jamie was the most inexperienced. Something his father had insisted on years ago, keeping a younger man on the council. *Everyone must be heard*, his father had said.

"I accept. And tonight, a wedding will take place. Spare no expense or effort. I doona wish my lovely bride to mistake her wedding for a simple celebration. She must know what is expected of her. Clan MacKay has a new laird and lady."

The council and Petro applauded.

Fools. If they only knew what Alex had given up, how many of his dreams had been stripped away in the few days he'd been home. As he stood, the members surrounded him, offering congratulations. Alex graciously received their well wishes. He needed all the blessings he could get.

Petro embraced him, slapping his back. "A wise decision. And as all of these fine men have done, I, too, pledge my life to you, Alexander."

"Good," Alex said. "Take five men and ride to the beach. Bring my warriors home. I wish them to stay in the Highlands."

"Even Nasim, Kuresh, and Cyrus?"

"Especially them."

"Alex..." Petro started. "Few from this part of the world have set eyes on men from Constantinople. I am from Italy and stand out."

"I doona care. They are essential to my success."

"They are slaves."

"Nay," Alex said. "They are freemen as of today. I will reward their loyalty with lands and wives."

Petro approved of his choice and bowed. "As ye wish, Laird Alex."

HOURS AFTER HER conversation at the loch with Alex, Keely flatly refused to eat a bite or to allow Leah to help her into the beautiful gown meant for her wedding. "I'd rather starve to death and have birds peck away at my innards than marry a man I doona know."

The maid sighed. "If I could help ye escape, I would, Lady Keely. But Laird Alex has doubled the guard at yer door and around the keep. I believe he intends to make sure ye fulfill yer duty this time."

"This time..." she mocked, not meaning to slight Leah. "I am sorry. Tis nothing against ye."

"I understand."

"I am tired of men deciding where I can go and what I must do." She sat on the edge of the bed, gazing across the chamber to the hearth. "Men are more destructive than fire, the source of all the misery in the world."

"Do ye really think so?" Leah crawled behind her with a comb, sat down, and began to smooth the tangles out of her curls. The lass had gentle hands.

"Is there any other creature on God's earth that can so easily crush ye?"

"I-I doona know, milady. I've never considered such things."

"Think of the oppressed and suffering."

"Is that what ye consider yerself?"

A fair question. Keely scooted out of reach, hugging her center, contemplating an honest answer. When had life in the Highlands been easy for anyone? At least she was the daughter of a prosperous laird and clan. She'd never gone a day without food or shelter. There were always clean, warm clothes and shoes for her to choose from. Servants did her bidding. Guards protected her. Nay, she'd misspoken out of anger.

"Forgive me, Leah. I am fortunate. War is the fault of men. And the innocents who get killed or displaced as a result of their violence are the true victims of oppression and suffering."

Leah nodded. "Aye. Laird John always welcomed those without a home—cared for the sick and helpless—fed and clothed orphans—and never mistreated his servants. Some men are kind and gentle. I hope Laird Alex will be the same."

Keely swallowed the less-than-favorable opinion she had of Alexander MacKay. Why destroy the lass' hope? In all fairness, Keely couldna say what kind of laird Alex would be; she could only judge him based on the way he'd treated her. But there were reasons for his actions. Good reasons. Things she must accept responsibility for. And John, too. They'd both failed Alex in the worst way imaginable. Did it come as any surprise that he despised her? Tears burned her eyes.

"Lady Keely?" Leah squeezed her shoulder. "I willna let anyone harm ye."

Keely sniffled. "Thank, ye. Ye're the only friend I have here."

"In time," the maid offered, "the other women will acknowledge how good ye truly are."

"Let us talk of something else. No one has told me what man I am expected to marry."

Leah's demeanor changed immediately.

"Leah? Do ye know something?"

The maid shook her head.

"Please."

"I am sworn to secrecy, milady," she said.

It wouldna be fair to press the girl. "What *can* ye tell me?"

"The great hall has been transformed into a lovely sight," Leah said. "Wreaths of heather, candles, and bouquets of flowers for every lass. Laird Alex called for the silver to be cleaned and used for the feast table. The kitchens are bustling with twice the number of servants—Cook feels like a king, I think. He's never felt so important. There's boar and venison, even a lamb for the high table. The sweetest wine and best ale have been brought up from the cellar. All of the captains and their families have been invited, and there will be meat for all of the tenants and servants. Such generosity has not been seen here in a long time, Lady Keely."

Leah had described a joyous occasion, not a forced marriage between two strangers. Not her wedding feast. It couldna be. Why would Alex go to such lengths to please her? Then she remembered—Jamie was the likely groom. All of the fuss was over him. He deserved a memorable wedding. It dinna matter who the bride was.

The idea of spending her life with Jamie dinna disappoint her as much as it should. He was young and strong, well-thought of, handsome, a member of the council, and Alex's closest kinsman. The association with Alex did bother her. Every day for the rest of her life she'd have to see Alex—eat at his table, speak with him, listen to Jamie's stories about him, eventually meet the woman he'd fall in love with and marry, and children would follow ... many, she guessed. Alex's virility and passion had scarred Keely for life.

Any man she loved after would fall short of her expectations. If she could even love again. She wandered across the room to the hearth. She studied the beautiful tapestry crafted by Alex's mother. It captured the beauty and savagery of the MacKay holdings in every masterful stitch, down to the tartan-clad warriors guarding the north face of the keep. Keely closed her eyes and tried to imagine where she fit in, if her future could be intertwined with the scene depicted in the tapestry.

Could she be happy here? Accept being married to the laird's heir until Alex produced his own son? Would she finally love again? Accept a second chance at life and grace? Because until now, she had been living in the shadows, hidden away at Dunrobin Castle, a secret even her sire hadn't known. Aye, he knew she was safe, but her location had been withheld. In the five years she'd been away, only three missives had been sent to her father. There'd never been a reply, only a verbal acknowledgement that he understood she was alive.

In this moment, Alex was offering her an olive branch, the right to walk free again, to be a wife, perhaps a mother, and to live as a MacKay. She looked back at Leah who sat patiently on the bed still.

"Is Jamie my intended?"

"Lady Keely, please doona force me to answer any questions about who the laird has chosen for ye."

Even if she could stomach the notion of marrying again—she struggled with what followed … the marriage bed. Heat spiraled up her body. Something so sacred should be shared with a man she loved. A man she chose, not someone Alex, her father, or anyone else designated.

"The gown." She attempted to focus on something else. "Show it to me, please."

A slow smile warmed Leah's face as she got up and retrieved the delicate dress from the back of a chair. The maid held it up. "The color suits ye."

Aye, light green wool with silver threading and silver beads. There were matching slippers on the floor. "Where is the bag I travelled with?"

"I put yer garments away already."

"I had jewels."

"Aye. In the chest over there." The maid pointed to the far wall where two trunks were situated.

The bag she'd managed to escape with had everything in the world she cared about, including an emerald and gold necklace and ring from her ma. If there was ever an occasion to wear the heirlooms, now would be an appropriate time. "Please bring the jewelry basket to me."

"But, milady, there is no need. Laird Alex has supplied a wedding gift for ye." Leah put the dress down and hurried to the table. She opened a box. "I have never seen anything so beautiful before."

Keely peered over her shoulder. Six breathtaking pieces awaited her approval, a necklace, ring, bracelet, brooch, and two hair combs. Each contained a brilliant ruby surrounded by gold and silver knotwork, set on gold. "This is a mistake, I am sure." Keely eyed the maid. "Return the gifts to Alex. Tell him I canna accept such expensive things."

"Nay," the maid insisted. "I wouldna dare. These are exquisite, Lady Keely, brought here from Constantinople."

Keely snorted. Why would Alex be travelling with women's jewelry? And where had he gotten the gown? Surely these were gifts meant for his favorite concubine. Jealousy burned inside of her, but she dismissed it. What Alex did and who he did it with, dinna matter. Her future husband waited belowstairs. A fateful decision must be made, either accept her place as a MacKay or fight for her freedom.

She trekked to the narrow window and looked about. Dusk was settling in. The hills surrounding the keep were in bloom. Twas the season of possibilities. Nature always renewed itself in the summer, so why shouldna Keely do the same? She hadna slept well in days, and that exhaustion had settled bone-deep. The desire to fight against Alex was fading. And if she left there, there were a limited number of places she could go.

The Sutherlands were out of the question. What about Clan Gunn? Or the Sinclairs? Perhaps the MacLeods? She adored Elizabeth MacLeod, the laird's youngest daughter. Nay—her presence would stir up trouble after she overstayed her welcome. The more she thought about it, even returning to her sire's house seemed impossible.

The convent. Only for a brief moment did she consider herself worthy of becoming a nun.

A knock on the chamber door startled Keely.

Leah hurried to open it.

"Tis time," a man said.

"Lady Keely isna ready."

"But Laird Alex..."

"Can wait a little longer," the maid finished for him and closed the door. She walked back to the table. "Lady Keely, what will ye have me do?"

There was another choice, one that required utter humility. She could request a meeting with Alex and beg for mercy—confess her deepest feelings for him. If he knew how she felt, surely, he wouldna marry her off to another man. He must care about her, he even told her he couldna imagine her with another man. But what kind of future could they share if it was built on regrets, anger, and lies?

She suddenly felt hot and her hands started to shake. Taking a last look about the bedchamber, she knew there was no alternative but to marry. "Make me a beautiful bride."

Chapter Twelve

LOW ON PATIENCE, Alex kept close watch of the entrance to the great hall. He finished off another cup of ale and wiped his mouth with the back of his hand. Keely should have been there by now. Aye, women were afforded extra time, especially on their wedding night, but he suspected she was doing this on purpose to prove a point.

A hundred guests waited with him, mainly his captains and their families, his cousins, Petro, and the soldiers from his ship. The general mood reflected excitement and curiosity about the bride, for everyone knew Keely had no idea who waited to marry her. A necessary tactic to keep her from trying to escape. The lass loathed him and would never consent to wed him.

He'd celebrate their nuptials, drink and dance with her, and when it came time to go abovestairs, he'd do so with eagerness. She'd belonged to him from the day she pledged her heart and soul to him. And by divine right, according to Father Michael, Alex had been brought home from Constantinople to claim her.

The lutes and harp filled the room with sweet sound, as did the laughter of his guests. But none of it could soothe the beast within him. The celebration couldna resurrect the joy he'd felt all those years ago when he was a lad in love. Keely had consumed him body and soul with one smile and words of devotion. Her raven hair and blue eyes bewitched him then, and if he wasn't vigilant, could do so now. For the lady had the face of an angel but the heart of a witch.

Just as he was about to take up another cup of ale, the guards assigned to her chamber door appeared at the entrance of the great hall. Behind them stood Father Michael and Leah. A head taller than most men, Alex still strained to catch sight of his bride through the throng. When the guards finally stepped aside, a lass handed Leah a bouquet of flowers, and Father Michael took up his position at the front of the room.

Alex couldna breathe after he spotted Keely in the gown he'd carefully chosen. The soft material clung to her curves, the ruby necklace sparkled in the torchlight at her throat, and the red stones in the combs she wore in her unbound, waist-length hair captivated him. Everything about her made him wild and dangerous. But nothing pleased him more than the idea that she was about to be bound to him by the holiest of oaths in front of enough witnesses that she could never challenge the validity of their marriage. The little bird had been caught and her wings clipped.

Father Michael silenced the musicians, and Alex strutted across the room, full of pride and confidence. He stopped in front of the priest. The crowd parted to let Leah and Keely closer.

"Harlot!" someone screamed.

"Stop this unholy alliance," another called.

"Ye canna marry yer brother's wife!"

Madness unraveled inside Alex, and he drew his sword. He'd silence their contemptuous tongues forever. Angus's death hadn't served as a strong enough deterrent. There was plenty of room on the outer wall for more pikes and heads.

The agitators had gained access to the great hall through the main doors. And as Alex got closer, he recognized several of the men—Angus's supporters.

Mathe and Jamie were at his side, clearing a path through the crowd.

"We demand justice!" the obvious leader said. "Come back to Christ, Laird Alex, pick a chaste wife from among our daughters."

"Shut yer bloody mouth, Levi," Alex spat as he bludgeoned the man with the hilt of his sword.

Levi stumbled backward, his brow bleeding profusely. "I am unarmed, but unafraid to die for what is right."

Alex handed his weapon to Jamie. "And now I am unarmed."

Blood blurred Levy's vision, but he dinna relent. "That woman…" he pointed at Keely who had made her way to the doors. "Is an abomination. A witch. She is responsible for Laird John's death."

Alex growled like an animal and lunged. He knocked Levi off his feet and they rolled, Alex landing on top of him. Straddling his chest, he'd give the naysayer one chance to take back his words.

"Ye have a death wish?" Alex asked.

"I have the truth." Levi spat in his face, which unleashed Alex's rage.

He punched him repeatedly—crushing his nose and breaking his jaw. "*Marbhphaisg ort*!" Alex would gladly provide Levi's death shroud.

"Alex!" Jamie tried to pull him off Levi.

But Alex wouldna stop.

"Laird Alex, the man is half dead already," Father Michael admonished. "Please, for the sake of yer bride, show restraint."

As he raised his fist, Keely's tiny hand covered his. "Alex."

He gazed up at her, sure he looked like a berserker covered

in his enemy's blood.

"Ye have defended my honor. Let Jamie deal with him now."

Something about the way she gazed at him, the soft but firm sound of her voice, and the fact that she'd maintained her composure in the face of such violence on her wedding night, allowed him to think clearly again. He'd stop for her and no one else.

Alex slowly stood up.

"Get the bastard out of my sight," he said.

Jamie signaled for two other guards to assist him.

Once the men were removed, Alex turned his full attention to Keely. She seemed unbelievably calm for what she'd just witnessed. He bowed out of embarrassment for not safeguarding her properly. No woman should be exposed to such violence. "I am sorry for what those men accused ye of, Keely. Are ye all right?"

She dinna say anything for a long moment, but peered across the great hall, taking in the decorations and the finely set high table. "I am unharmed, Alex. But something troubles me more than anything those men could say. Are ye my groom?"

"Aye."

"Why dinna ye tell me at the loch?"

In a rare moment of tenderness, Alex caressed her cheek. "We were interrupted, remember?"

"Ye had plenty of time to disclose such an important detail about tonight."

"I wish I hadna been so selfish, Keely. Sometimes my temper gets the best of me, as it does any man who's been wronged."

"So ye wanted to hurt me?" Her voice was tremulous.

"Nay," he said. "I wanted to spend some time with ye, see if ye'd changed yer mind about staying here. Tis better to have a willing bride."

"I know this isna very easy for either of us."

"But we are both here."

"Aye," she said. "I had two choices, accept this marriage or escape. I'm tired of running."

"I canna promise ye love, lass, but I can give ye comfort and pleasure—and protect ye."

"Ye doona love me?"

Why did she have to gaze at him with those lovely blue eyes at a moment like this? Most men would lie about their feelings. But he dinna want to build their marriage on falsehoods. "I care about ye, lass."

"'Tis a start."

"Aye. Give me yer hand, Keely."

He twined his fingers through hers, ready to stand before the priest and exchange vows.

"Yer tunic is ruined," Keely pointed out.

Alex looked down at his clothes. Aye, he looked the part of a bloodthirsty Highland laird. All the better, for he must deal with the other men who had accompanied Levi into the hall. "If ye'll be patient, there is one more thing I must do." She nodded, and he turned his attention to the waiting offenders. "Rebels," he said. "How dare ye disturb the peace in my home."

The six men dropped to their knees.

"Please," one of the men begged, "have mercy on us."

"We dinna mean to hurt anyone, milord," another said.

"Mercy…" two more cried in unison.

He scoffed. "Did ye show mercy?"

Silence enveloped the great hall.

"I willna tolerate such behavior. Ye falsely accused my bride and dishonored the clan with yer filthy lies. Ye screamed for justice. And ye'll have it. Mathe!"

"Milord?" The captain stood at attention.

"Bind these men and take them to a cell. Let them rot."

"Aye."

"After I am married, perhaps we shall sacrifice them to whatever god or devil ye want. For they are not worthy of living another day."

The crowd gasped. The days of ruling this clan with a light hand was over. John had done them a great disservice. Alex loved his people: he'd die for any man, woman, or child, but he wouldna tolerate uprisings of any sort.

"Father Michael," Alex said. "Get on with the nuptials." No more delays. Alex watched his beautiful bride with renewed interest. She'd shown grace and courage.

Alex had instructed the priest to keep the ceremony brief. There must be no misunderstandings. The vows would include her promise to be submissive. And in turn, he'd protect her, *always*.

"Lord Alexander Joseph MacKay, repeat after me. With the Almighty as our witness, and in front of these good people, I do take Keely Marie Oliphant as my wife, pledge my faith in body and spirit, promise to be loyal and kind, pledge my strength and goods in sickness and health, in whatever condition the Lord will place me, until in death we do part."

Alex dinna hesitate. He'd have this woman—to tame like he would the wildest mare.

Keely held his gaze as she recited her vow.

"With the Almighty as our witness, I do take Alexander Joseph MacKay as my husband, pledge my faith in body and spirit, promise to honor him as laird and master, to remain obedient, and swear fealty to Clan MacKay. I pledge my life in sickness and health, in whatever condition the Lord will place me, until in death we do part."

Alex slipped a delicate gold band on Keely's finger, sealing their union.

After a short prayer, the priest tied their right hands together with a strip of MacKay tartan, then laid his hands on their heads. "May the Almighty keep and bless ye forever."

The crowd cheered.

"Ye may kiss the bride, Laird Alex," Father Michael announced.

Alex tugged Keely into his arms, not giving her time to think. He captured her mouth with his, and to his delight, her lips parted. Their tongues swirled together in urgent need. His grip tightened about her, and she leaned into him, kissing him back—threatening his tight control. Nay, the lass wouldna steal his sanity.

He pulled back, desperate to taste her again. "Aye, lass," he muttered. "Tis a promise of what's to come. What should have happened long ago. I will make ye a woman tonight, Keely. And if I'm blessed, maybe plant my first son inside ye." She made his pikk as hard as a steel rod.

The musicians began to play again, and Alex steered his bride to the high table. "Drink and eat," he suggested warmly. "Ye'll need yer strength this eve, and every night in the foreseeable future."

NOTHING FELT REAL. Even with her groom smiling at her—she still couldna wrap her mind around it. The man she had always loved, wept for, missed every day of her five-year absence, was her husband now. A dream come true, with one striking difference—he dinna love her. Hearing those words come out of his mouth broke her heart but dinna dissuade her in the least.

She'd willingly taken him as her husband. That's how it always should have been. His denial only made her more determined to win his heart back.

As much as he carried on about how she belonged to him, they truly belonged to each other. Alex raised his cup and toasted her beauty. The crowd followed suit, blessing their marriage.

"When will ye let my father know about our marriage."

"I have already dispatched a messenger."

That surprised her. "He willna be happy about it."

"What is the worst thing that can happen? God and the law are on our side, lass. Though I will rue the day he shows up here."

She sighed and rested her elbows on the table. Aye, her father and brothers would come after her once they found out. Laird Oliphant dinna like being made a fool of.

"Doona fash, Keely. I will deal with him."

"I believe ye," she said. "But it doesna make it any easier for me. He will see my time with the Sutherlands as a black mark on his name."

Alex shushed her and kissed her cheek. "Think about it tomorrow. Tonight, we celebrate."

"I will try."

"Good," he said. "Taste the lamb."

After she ate the tenderest morsels of meat Alex had cut, the servants brought out platters of sweet bread, cheese, fresh fruit, and more wine. The best she'd ever tasted.

"Where did this wine come from?" she asked Alex.

"Italy."

"How many times have ye visited that country?"

"Many times."

"Is the sea as warm and blue as rumored?'

"Aye," he said. "As blue and fathomless as yer eyes. As hot as our bed will be tonight."

His answer made her blush. Though she had never been with a man, she often wondered what Alex would look like naked. He'd inspired countless fantasies on many a lonely night. Now she had the right to touch and kiss him. She covered her mouth, ashamed of her impure thoughts. Such things weren't appropriate for a maiden to consider, but he made it difficult to not think about it. Every time he gazed at her, it was as if he was undressing her with his eyes.

"Ye look beautiful in the rubies, lass."

"Thank ye," she said. "I doona deserve such gifts, Alex."

"Keep the jewelry. There will be times such luxuries are necessary to wear."

Keely touched the stone at her throat. "Nay," she said again. "After tonight, please take them back."

"I willna." He took a drink of wine.

Why did he insist she keep them? "Did ye sail to Scotland with the intent of getting married?"

Alex signaled for a servant to refill his cup. "Nay. I came here to see John and to provide the necessary gold for him to hire mercenaries to protect our assets, nothing more."

"Why were ye in possession of such jewels?"

He chuckled at her question. "Does it matter?"

"I know about yer concubines, Alex."

He waved a hand dismissively. "I am not the kind of man to hide anything, lass. Ye should know that already. The clan is fully aware of who and what I am, where I've lived and how I lived. Men have needs, and in Constantinople, sex is not something men are ashamed of. It's considered a matter of good health."

Keely nearly choked at the absurdity of his explanation. "A

matter of good health? Like eating enough food or having warm clothes to wear?"

"Aye."

He actually believed what he was saying. "And now?"

"The only thing that has changed is I have a wife to share my bed with."

"What if I want a separate chamber?"

"Nay. Ye will sleep with me every night." He covered her hand with his. "Ye willna want to be apart from me once we spend our first night together, lass. I am a generous lover. I'll never hurt ye or force ye to do anything ye are uncomfortable with."

The words stole her breath. She believed him, but the thought of him still owning concubines, even if they were thousands of miles away, left her unhappy. "Who does this jewelry belong to?"

He sighed. "If ye must know, they were intended for Layla, my favorite concubine."

Keely pushed her chair back from the table, intending to leave the great hall.

Alex wouldna let her, he gripped her upper arm and shook his head. "Ye willna leave the celebration. In the future, think before ye ask such questions."

"I had my suspicions about it already. I am sure my dress was a gift for another woman. Perhaps ye could still send it to her." She'd meant as a way to lighten the mood but it had come out sounding more severe.

Alex grimaced. "I doona want to hear another word on the matter."

"Will ye keep the women, then?"

"Do ye wish me to bring them here?"

His arrogance made her angry. Would she ever be enough to satisfy him? She knew little about the art of lovemaking. His eyes flickered with amusement, but she dinna find it entertaining at all. "Send for yer women," she said boldly. "As long as ye doona prevent Struan Sutherland from joining us, too."

The menacing look on Alex's face told her she'd given him a taste of the humiliation she'd felt. How else would he learn to respect her feelings?

"What did ye say?" he asked through gritted teeth.

"If ye intend to bring yer concubines here, it would only be right if I were allowed to have a lover, too."

He tugged her close. "What are ye saying, lass? Ye've had relations with Struan?"

"What do ye mean by relations?"

"Would ye like me clear the high table of all its succor, spread ye out, and show ye what I mean?"

One thing became abundantly clear, her husband cared. How much, she dinna know. But his possessiveness meant there was hope for their marriage. "If ye wish, my laird."

He loosened his grip on her wrist, then gulped down a generous amount of wine. "Ye need to watch yer tongue, lass. If I..."

"Laird and Lady MacKay..."

Alex growled at the interruption as Petro bowed.

"In the eastern lands we offer gifts to the bride," the scholar said.

Keely leaned close to Alex and whispered, "I wonder who these treasures are really meant for."

Alex snorted. "Be quiet, my sweet."

She smiled at Petro.

"Who offers these gifts?" Alex asked.

"Let me be the first to congratulate your beautiful bride—and to wish the both of you every happiness." Petro climbed the dais stairs, leaving a bolt of scarlet colored silk on the table in front of Keely. "To match the color of the stones you wear."

Keely had never seen such fine material. Her fingers glided over smooth cloth. "Thank ye," she said.

"Did Laird Alexander tell you what the color red represents in the east, Lady Keely?"

"Nay," she answered.

"Vigor and virility," he informed her. "It's also believed to increase a man's appetite."

The people nearby chuckled, and she could only guess what they were thinking—perhaps the same as her. Petro wasn't referring to the kind of appetite that made a man eat more bread; he clearly meant sex.

"Ye are very kind," she said.

"If I may," he continued, "there are several admirers who wish to thank you for inviting them to your wedding."

A man with skin the color of the earth stepped forward. He wore a loose-fitting tunic, leather braes, and boots. His hair and eyes were even darker than Petro's. A curved sword like Alex's and several knives were secured on his weapon belt.

"May I present, Cyrus Bin Kalil and his brothers, Kuresh and Nasim—all sons of Kalil, a lord of Constantinople."

The handsome men bowed, and Cyrus joined Petro on the dais, offering her a blue stone. "Sapphire, the color of your eyes," he said in perfect Gaelic with a strange accent. "I wish you joy and many sons."

Kuresh followed, presenting her with an emerald, and then Nasim, who offered her a bag filled with gold coins.

Careful to appreciate each gift, she dinna know how to thank them. "I am humbled—truly grateful. How can I…"

Alex stood. "What my wife wishes to say, is she would be honored to dance with ye." He waved his hand at the musicians. "Play—I want to hear music and see everyone dancing."

"Alex … I…"

"Ye will entertain these men, Keely. And when ye finish, I will have *my* dance."

Chapter Thirteen

"DO YE STILL deny your feelings for the girl, Alex?" Petro asked.

Alex had removed himself from the high table and chosen a spot near the main hearth. Though he enjoyed talking with his friend, he was only half listening. His beautiful bride commanded most of his attention as she danced with the brothers from Constantinople.

Petro's question grated on his nerves like stone on metal. "I have feelings." He'd told the scholar that many times already.

"Why not share those feelings with her? It will help."

"Help what?"

"Settle things between you. I saw you arguing with her, Alex."

"Ye're a nosey bastard, Petro."

"And you're drunk, Alex."

"I'm many things this night," Alex said. As for being drunk, the ale helped calm him. After nearly killing Levi with his bare hands, he couldna possibly take Keely upstairs and be gentle. Nay, he needed time to recover from the violence. And a blasted bath. He'd washed his face at the high table, but the stench of blood had stayed on his clothes.

"Have I ever failed you?" Petro asked.

"Why do ye ask? Ye're like a woman who constantly needs

reassurance about her place in my heart. Shall I speak of my love for ye?" Alex leaned over like he wanted to kiss his friend.

"Christ." Petro pushed him away. "I am not jesting. Whenever I offer guidance about Keely, you wave me aside as if my words do not matter."

"I've spent five years planning it, and never believed it would actually happen."

"That's what I'm afraid of, Alex. What you will say and do once you get her alone."

"I am not a fool. My future success with the clan depends heavily on Keely. Her skills at running a household are very valuable. She's a capable lass, and I will make sure she knows it."

"Tis a start," Petro said.

"She already asked me if I loved her."

"What did you say?"

"I told her the truth, that I cared."

From his position, he could see most of the great hall. Both of their gazes followed Keely's lithe form as she passed by, stepping gracefully to the music.

"Your feelings are undeniable, Alexander. I see it in your eyes whenever you watch her. That is not the look of a man merely in lust. It is the heat of love, of keeping what you once lost."

"And what do ye know of such things? Ye stick yer pikk in anything with legs."

Petro chuckled. "My taste is more discriminating."

"And I shall never be critical of yer needs, my friend, as ye shouldna harp on me about mine."

"I understand, but a miserable union will destroy a man's house."

Alex's eyes sparkled with mischief. "This house is built upon rock." He held his fist up, symbolizing the erection beneath his tartan. "I willna deny the lass anything, Petro. She will feel the extent of my passion—the years I've tried to extinguish it with the empty kisses of foreign women."

Though his head was swimming with hot memories about Keely, Alex refused to surrender to the tender feelings in his heart. Aye, he cared—more than he should. A tiny ember of what he used to feel for the lass had ignited inside him the day he encountered her in the great hall for the first time—how she came forward and called his name in front of his captains and tenants. That fierceness in her eyes, the willingness to aid his cause. The Oliphants were worthy allies. But he couldna trust her. She'd broken his heart. She'd forsaken her own father by running away.

If he let his guard down, she'd find a way inside his mind and heart—stealing his very soul. The fact that she still had that kind of power over him represented something he dinna want to think about, *ever*.

"What are you afraid of, Alex?"

The question caused Alex to set his empty cup on the mantle. He rested his palm against the stone wall and stared into the flames. Drinking himself numb was futile. Nothing could erase the past—even temporarily. Nay—his feelings were too intense to forget—too real. He'd promised himself that he'd shield the lass from harm, but when it came to what existed between them outside the bedchamber, she deserved a bitter portion—to feel what he'd felt, to suffer as he had.

"I fear nothing, and wish to speak of this no more. Go and pick a lass to dance with and leave me in peace."

That caused his friend to raise a brow. "You changed your mind about me wooing the maids?"

"I canna forbid ye from bedding a lass. But I give ye fair warning … get one with child, and ye will find yerself standing before Father Michael as quickly as I did."

Petro's gaze searched the crowd. "The redheaded girl…"

"Which one?"

He gestured toward the doorway which opened into the kitchens. "The buxom one."

"Ye've a liking for Glenna. Her sire tragically died at my brother's side."

"I am sorry for the loss."

"As am I. But Glenna and her sister Erin will need husbands to provide for them."

"I am not opposed to the idea of marriage, Alex."

"Then pursue the lass with my blessing."

"She will need time to mourn the loss of her father."

"Glenna needs comfort."

"As do you," his friend reminded him.

"Is every word I say an opportunity for ye to use it against me?"

"Only if it serves a purpose."

"Then maybe I should carve yer tongue out."

The both laughed. Alex appreciated the blunt way Petro expressed himself. That's why he made the best adviser and friend.

Nasim approached with Keely, then bowed. "Thank you for the honor of dancing with your wife."

Alex nodded. "Bring yer brothers to the high table, Nasim. I have news to share."

"I will get them." Nasim bowed once more and departed.

"If you will excuse me, Lady Keely, Alex, I wish to speak with someone," Petro said.

Alex gave his friend a knowing smile. Glenna was standing at a nearby table. If she kept his friend occupied, it would spare Alex from getting more lectures.

"Did ye enjoy the music?" Alex asked his wife.

"Aye—all three brothers are excellent dancers and pleasant to speak with." Keely paused. "Is it true, Alex?'

"What, lass?"

"The brothers are yer slaves?'

"Aye."

"B-but..."

"Doona judge me for keeping the ways of foreigners when I lived in their land."

"It goes against everything we Scots believe in. The Almighty endowed *all* men with certain attributes—being a slave isna one of them."

"Yer concern is appreciated but unwarranted."

Her look told him she'd never agree.

Alex sighed at the need to further explain himself. "Are we not slaves to the crown? From the poorest tenant to the highest chieftain?"

She considered it. "In a way. We are the king's subjects."

"It means the same thing, lass. And if ye must know, I spared the life of their father when I was paid to kill him. He waged war against a rival lord and lost. Twas left to my discretion to do with his life as I wished. As I raised my sword, Lord Kalil made an offer I couldna refuse. His three eldest sons in exchange for his life. Such an offer is only made to an enemy a man respects."

"That's a terrible fate for his sons."

"Again, doona judge their ways by our own. They are an ancient race. And when such an arrangement is made, they must be treated in a certain way—as sons of a prince."

"They are princes?"

"Aye. They fight with me and receive an equal portion of the rewards we gain by defeating our enemies. The gifts offered to ye were from their own wealth. Slaves have certain rights,

Keely, regardless of their high or low birth."

"I am sorry for misjudging ye without knowing the whole truth."

Alex escorted his wife back to the high table where Nasim and his brothers waited. Once seated, Alex called for silence.

"In Constantinople, on a man's wedding day, he is expected to share his good fortune. A tradition not too far from our own. So, on this momentous occasion, I will keep this practice alive."

The crowd cheered and raised their cups.

Alex did the same, taking a drink of ale. "Cyrus, Kuresh, and Nasim, sons of Kalil, princes in their own right, ye have served me well."

The brothers raised their cups. "We salute you, Laird Alexander."

"Such loyalty and bravery deserve freedom," Alex said.

"Freedom?" Cyrus asked quietly. "What do you mean?"

Alex leaned across the table. "Yer father's debt to me is satisfied. Walk among men again as an equal."

"All of us?" Nasim asked.

"Aye."

"What if we wish to serve you still?" Kuresh asked.

"Then I willna send ye away. Ye will be appointed to my personal guard and honored as a MacKay."

"A MacKay?" Kuresh asked. "You wish me to take yer surname?"

"If ye choose to stay here, aye. Ye canna live in the past," Alex said, relying on the wise words of his scholar. "There is time to consider yer futures, to make a choice."

The brothers bowed.

"Any man who questions my decision and mistreats ye, will feel my rage as Angus did when he laid hands on my bride."

The guests cheered and called out the brothers' names.

"Today marks a new beginning for Clan MacKay. I wish my father and brother were here to celebrate with us." Alex turned to Keely. "And now, if ye doona mind, I will take my bride abovestairs."

Before she could protest, Alex scooped her up and made his way through the happy throng.

"God's blessings," some called.

"Bolt the door from the inside and out," a man warned. "The lass might run away."

"Be at peace, Laird Alexander, and get Lady Keely with child, that will keep her a MacKay."

Though he appreciated the well wishes, the words stung his pride. The only thing that would keep his young wife in their bed was him. She had been left a maiden too long and dinna know her rightful place, dinna understand what being a wife meant.

Keely wrapped her arms around his neck.

"Are ye afraid, lass?"

"Nay." She peeked up at him. "Are ye?"

He stopped mid-stair and laughed. "Ye'll never give me peace, Keely. For almost every word out of yer pretty mouth surprises me."

"Blame my father, he taught me everything I know."

Alex dinna want her to lose the fire in her belly. Even though he complained about her being stubborn and disobedient, he'd have grown bored with a submissive wife. And that fighting spirit would eventually win the hearts of Clan MacKay back. Keely dinna face an easy future, but he knew she would rise above the challenges.

"After tonight, lass, there will be no more confusion left between us, I promise." He pushed the bedchamber door open with the toe of his boot.

ONCE SHE AND Alex were inside, he barred the door, then turned to her. "Later, men will be posted outside the door and below, in case ye'd be foolish enough to jump out of the window."

She lifted her chin. "Ye still have no faith in me?" She couldna blame him for being overly cautious. The past still weighed heavily on them both. In time she'd prove herself trustworthy again.

Alex walked to the hearth. He stoked the fire with a metal poker. "I know ye well, Keely. That alone gives me every right to be suspicious. But I am willing to set our differences aside and start our lives together. There are many things I like about ye."

She sighed, taking in the surroundings, including the enormous bed she was sure generations of MacKay lairds and their ladies had slept in. Surely it was large enough to accommodate Alex and three or four women at one time. She frowned at the thought.

"Just then," Alex pointed out, "a shadow crossed yer face. Why?"

"Tis nothing."

"Tell me at once," he demanded.

"A foolish notion, nothing more."

"I will decide what's foolish, lass."

"The bed..."

Alex gazed at it. "Is it not to yer liking?"

"It will serve," she said.

"Keely..."

"Perhaps ye, me, *and* the rest of yer women."

Alex hung the poker on its hook, then crossed the room to where she stood.

"I have *six* concubines, Keely."

She pivoted away from him and drew closer to the bed, imagining eight bodies tucked beneath the sheets and furs. "I'm afraid it will be a rather tight fit, milord."

"What?"

"Can ye no picture it? Look closely."

Alex stood next to her.

"Ye would surely prefer the middle. And I will sleep to yer right, as is my proper place, and Layla, yer favorite concubine, will sleep to yer left. I'm afraid the rest will have to fight for their positions. I doona want the responsibility of keeping track of such things."

Alex gaped at her. "Keely…"

"I am not happy about it, Alex. I have no choice but to accept the unnatural cravings ye developed in that strange land."

"Keely."

"Is Layla beautiful?"

"She is nothing next to ye."

"What about the… What did ye say?"

"Layla pales in comparison to ye, Keely. All of them do."

Her heart raced at the rare compliment from Alex. "I-I…"

Alex reached for her hands, cradling them in his. "Did ye not listen to the vow I took belowstairs? Pledging my body to ye?"

"Of course I did. How many men have spoken the same words at their wedding only to break their sacred vow soon after? If I had a choice, I wouldna be here, *we* wouldna be here." She started to panic, fear of the unknown growing inside her. How could she trust Alex? It seemed they shared common concerns. And a marriage built on anything but trust was doomed, was it not? "Tis not too late to send me back to my father." She couldna hide the tears in her eyes. "Please…"

Alex frowned and released her hands. "Keely. Ye disappoint me greatly. Where is the brave woman I married, the one who dinna stumble over her words in front of Father Michael, who accepted her future as my wife?"

"Ye dinna give me a choice!"

"Aye, I did."

"When?"

"Did anyone force ye into that gown? Make ye stand in front of the priest and my captains? Ye spoke the words, lass—freely."

Keely covered her face with both hands, struggling to take a steady breath. "Ye threatened me, Alex. Made it abundantly clear that I had no choice but to marry the man ye'd chosen for me. I assumed it was Jamie, not ye."

"Would ye prefer my cousin?" His eyes narrowed.

"Alex! Why are ye playing games with me? Twisting my words—yer words? So much has happened these last few days. So much pain and death. How could I think clearly?"

"Lass," he started. "Whether ye know it or not, our fates were sealed long ago. The day we pledged ourselves to one another, was the day we were legally bound."

"What are ye saying?"

"Tis known as consent—like handfasting. Though we had no witnesses, we spoke the words before God. Yer marriage to John was invalid."

"I doona believe it." Feeling faint, she sat on the edge of the mattress, her slippered feet dangling over the floor.

"I dinna accept it very easily either, lass. But Petro is gifted in many ways. He understands law. If ye doubt my word, ye are welcome to summon him to this chamber and question him thoroughly."

"Now?"

"Aye."

She hugged herself, the weight of all these complications, of this new and unknown world, bearing down on her. She felt like she wanted to vomit. "There is no need. I've never known ye to be a liar, Alex." She met his gaze. "This is a cruel outcome for both of us, I think."

"Cruel?" he repeated. "Unfair, maybe. But not cruel."

"Ye had other plans for yer future, as did I. Hopes and dreams."

"Aye." He looked about the chamber. "Never did I think to come back here to serve as laird. Only to confront my brother for his betrayal."

"But I thought..."

"Aye, lass. And to give him gold as I said before. I may find it difficult to forgive him for marrying ye, but he's still a MacKay, still my only brother."

His words only added to her burden. She had played a part in that betrayal, even if her sire and Laird MacKay, Alex's father, had left her with no choice but to marry John. "Will ye ever forgive me?"

"Ye doona want to hear my answer, Keely."

"But I do."

Their gazes locked. His green eyes were so intense and cold.

"Forgiveness. Trust. Love. Tenderness. None of these things are necessary to have a successful marriage."

"Ye are very wrong."

"Nay, I am not."

"Aye, ye are," she countered. Convincing Alex of anything seemed impossible, but it dinna mean she had to accept his heartless idea of marriage.

He released a mirthless laugh that cut through her. "This isna a fairytale, Keely."

He was strong. He was brave. He was handsome. And he was Laird MacKay now. But he wasna happy. Maybe if she dedicated her time to changing his mind...

"Shall I show ye what makes a fruitful match?"

Did she have a choice in the matter?

Before she could answer, Alex stepped between her legs, towering over her, the passion in his expression unmistakable. She held her breath as he cradled her face between his big hands and tilted her head upward. He lowered his lips to hers, gently kissing her quivering mouth. The contact made her tingle all over. But her instinctual defenses made her keep her lips tightly sealed. One kiss from him could change everything. And she couldna hold her breath much longer!

He chuckled and drew back. "Is this yer idea of a kiss, Keely?"

"I-I…"

As soon as she spoke, he struck, his masculine scent and taste consuming her as his tongue swept over hers. His hand slipped underneath her hair to her nape and locked her in place. And against her better judgment, she returned that kiss with equal hunger—with desperate need to be wanted. Five long years hadn't extinguished her inner fire for Alex. With one flick of his tongue, one touch, she transformed into the wanton maiden she used to be whenever he was close. Only this time, the happiness that bubbled up inside her in the past was sadly gone.

She blamed her nerves—or too much wine—or maybe this was her future. A loveless marriage built on raw lust. A man dinna need to love a woman to get her with child.

"Keely," he whispered, as he gently urged her to lie back on the bed.

She dinna resist, and he climbed atop her, his knees planted on either side of her body. She gazed up at him, a new wave of emotions assailing her, fear and fascination causing her heart to race. He had noble features and would sire beautiful children. Physically beautiful, but with hearts of stone…

The spell was broken, and Keely struggled to push him off her. "Away from me," she demanded.

It did little good; he dinna move.

"Did ye hear me?"

"Aye." He folded his arms across his chest.

"Ye canna keep me here!"

He threw his head back and laughed deeply—irritatingly so. "Ye're my wife, lass, I can do whatever I wish with ye. And in case ye forgot, that door is barred from the inside and out. We are stuck here *together*."

Chapter Fourteen

THE MORE SHE denied and fought against their mutual hunger, the more desirable his new wife became. Color suffused Keely's lovely cheeks, and those damnable blue eyes reminded him of the burning sun over the desert. He had no intention of forcing her or hurting her—but she must understand what was going to happen tonight. The marriage *must* be consummated. He couldna live two lives—his heart in Constantinople and his mind in the Highlands. Nay, he needed to become her husband in every way in order to find the anchor necessary to keep him in Scotland. His ship was still conveniently located only a short ride away, ready to sail wherever he commanded.

"Ye're heavier than a blasted stone," she complained. "Get off me."

Alex had been very careful to balance most of his weight on his knees. She was searching for any excuse to get rid of him. "Nay."

She sighed. "What if I fall asleep with ye sitting there?"

"Then I will make special use of the time."

"What?" She sat up, leaning on her elbows.

"Did I stutter, lass?"

"Ye'd use me in such a way?"

Though he wanted to chuckle at her silly thought, he kept a

serious expression. "A man must do his duty."

"Please get off of me. I need a drink of wine."

"All right, lass. Since ye asked so nicely." He repositioned himself on the bed and watched as she scurried across the room to the table where food and drink had been left for them.

With shaky hands, she poured herself a measure of wine and gulped it down, then refilled her cup.

"Easy, lass," he advised. "If ye drink too much, it will take longer for me to do my duty."

She slammed the cup down and thrust a hand on her hip, looking infuriated and maybe a little drunk. "Ye and yer men can ride away from here, Alex. We're married as far as the church is concerned. Why stay when ye have so much to return to in Constantinople?"

Her easy dismissal angered him and he stood up. "And leave ye a virgin for another night? For the next man who wants ye?"

She clicked her tongue. "There isna a man left in the Highlands who would dare have me after everything that has transpired these last few days—after the humiliation I've suffered."

"Ye're wrong."

"Am I?"

He launched himself at her, capturing her in his arms, tasting her again and again, swallowing her bitterness and the remnants of the honey wine she'd just drank. "I am a man, Keely. Ye're husband."

Guiding her hand over his stomach and underneath his tartan, he made sure she felt his excitement. And when she feigned innocence and tried to yank her hand free, he whispered in her ear. "Nay, lassie. Doona act as if ye've never felt me before." For she had, many times under a starlit sky. They'd explored each other's bodies freely through their clothes, kissing and petting until he'd nearly lost his mind. But honor had held him back. And by God, since she was officially his wife now, there'd be no more teasing.

"A-Alex," she purred. She cupped his manhood and offered her mouth to him.

He tangled his free hand in her long hair, then kissed her wildly. Aye, he wanted her to melt in his arms, to beg for anything and everything he could give her. Though he knew her to be a maiden, Keely had never been shy.

He released her mouth and feathered light kisses down the column of her neck, then nipped and licked the delicate skin between her breasts. The gown hugged her curves perfectly, revealing the generous swell of her breasts. *His* breasts.

The more he kissed her, the more she arched into him. Alex took advantage of the opportunity, unlacing the front of her dress, until the bodice gaped open enough for him to shove the material of her shift aside. He reached out and stroked her cheek while admiring her flesh. Flesh he wanted to explore and taste. Especially her rose-colored nipple. And he did just that, circling her areola with his tongue. Breathless and weak-kneed, Alex had to hold Keely up.

"Will ye fight me now, lass?"

She shook her head, delightfully complaint and willing.

He smiled like a fool, a hungry fool at that. With little effort, he carried her to the bed. She fell back against the soft mattress. Then Alex stripped his shirt and tartan off, and his boots followed.

Candlelight filled the bedchamber, and Alex stayed still so Keely could inspect his body. Curiosity filled her eyes. But when her stare lingered on his cock, he couldna wait any longer. He lifted the hem of her gown, raising it above her hips. What greeted him made him salivate. The patch of dark hair crowning her womanhood and the sight of her slim thighs made it impossible to hold back. He cupped her arse with both hands, lifting her to his face.

He licked gently at first, her feminine scent and taste pleasing—intoxicating.

Keely buried her fingers in his hair, pleading for him to stop at the same time she pressed his head to her core. It made him smile inside, letting him know she wanted this—him—them.

"Alex. Please. What are ye doing?"

If she required further explanation... He let go of one of her arse cheeks and quickly sunk a finger inside her, stroking in rhythm with his tongue. Her legs stiffened and she cried out again and again. But he dinna relent. Nay, she would peak in his mouth, and then he'd steal her kisses, and lick her again.

Seconds later, a faint pulse started, and he sucked the little nub harder.

"Alex!"

Her body went rigid. Alex dinna stop caressing her, he welcomed her excitement. Once she stilled, the only sound in the chamber was her heavy breathing. He crawled up her spent body, finding her staring at the ceiling.

Words weren't necessary as he continued to unlace her gown. She lifted her body so he could slide it off her, helping him with her shift next, and finally kicking off her silk slippers.

A low moan escaped Alex as he drank in every inch of her naked form. Not one detail escaped his admiration. From the shape of her breasts, flat stomach, the flare of her hips, even the tiny scar on her left knee—it all belonged to him now. She belonged to him. And now that he'd tasted her, heard her cry his name, felt the pulse of her pleasure, all he could think about was burying himself inside her—claiming her and ending the pain from the past.

He'd have waited a hundred years to have her—for her sheath was wet and tight and made for his pikk. Just like her sweet mouth was made for his lips and tongue. "Stand up, lass."

She lowered her head, meeting his stare.

"Ye want me to get up?"

"Aye," he said huskily. "I want to see ye—*all* of ye."

She slowly climbed off the bed, standing before him.

Another man would have fallen in love with her at first sight, but another man wouldna have ever let her go. And he had, until tonight. He circled her, running his fingers over her warm skin, loving the velvety smoothness of her arms and back, the lines of her legs and that arse … that well-formed, delicious arse. Stopping behind her, he gripped his pikk and gave it a firm squeeze, groaning in need and pain. The image in his mind was filthy and purely animalistic, taking his bride in the same way a stallion mounts a mare.

He wrapped an arm about her waist, tugging her against him. The air around them crackled with dark desire. He kissed her neck, the top of her ear, licked her shoulder, and then pinched her nipples. Keely snaked her hand behind him, finding his cock and bollocks.

"Aye, lass. Touch me just like that. Give it a tender squeeze."

She did.

"Do ye know what it's like to wait so long, Keely? To dream of the night when all yer bloody dreams will come true?" Damn his weakness! He'd said too much, and it angered him. She must never know, dinna deserve to know how much he'd wanted her while he was away.

"Aye," she whispered. "Those same dreams plagued my sleep every night."

Her confession hit him in the heart. What he struggled to

keep inside, she offered without hesitation. True feelings for him.

"Do ye love me, lass?"

She made no reply, but continued to provoke him with her touch.

Love had no place in this bedchamber. It would only complicate his simple plan. Duty over love—an heir to secure his clan's future, that was all he owed Keely, his brother, sire, and the people celebrating in the great hall. That dinna mean he couldna enjoy getting his wife with child.

He walked Keely to the end of the bed, buried his face in her hair, and gathered her breasts in his hands. "Bend over the bed for me, lass. Spread those luscious legs for me."

Keely remained ever responsive and eager to please.

Alex positioned himself at her entrance, running his fingers down her back. Then he fanned her dark tresses out and the sweet smell of heather filled the air. Testing her readiness, he gently pushed the tip of his member inside her. Aye, she was still wet, very wet. He pulled out and ran his fingers over her slick entrance. She pressed against him, urging him inside her.

"I am ready, Alexander, and know what to expect."

She gripped the fur tightly, waiting.

"As ye wish, Wife."

It took four gentle thrusts to open her enough to submerge himself inside her. Keely cried out in pain and pleasure, but was quick to reassure him that she dinna want him to stop. Not that he could have. He thrust again and again, satisfying that selfish need to take her from behind, but then wanted more—much more.

He pulled out, flipped her over, and draped one of her legs over his shoulder. "I want to see yer beautiful face, Keely."

She cupped his cheek and nodded. "And I want to see yours,

Alex."

He pumped inside her again, this time with less resistance. Heat and wetness enveloped him, and he leaned forward and plundered her mouth—kissing her with a force he'd never experienced before. Keely dug her fingernails into his shoulder, her tongue wrestling with his, her lips tightly sealed over his mouth.

The moment she began to unravel, he, too, lost control. They both screamed in utter shock and pleasure, the years of waiting for fulfillment finally over.

WHEN SHE AWOKE sometime in the night, Keely slipped from underneath her husband's arm and padded to the other side of the chamber. She stopped in front of the hearth where the fire still burned warm and bright. Something magical had occurred between them, something she couldna quite explain yet. After their first joining, he washed her with a soft, wet cloth, and then cleaned himself before crawling underneath the furs with her. Then he made love to her again, less frenzied this time, but with the same care for her pleasure.

Neither said a word as they drifted into sleep, but she remembered hearing his steady breathing, even a soft snore before she faded.

Just to prove Alex's words, she walked to the door and slid the bolt back, seeing if it would open. As he'd warned, the door was locked from the outside. She couldna get away even if she wanted to. Turning back toward the bed, she knew why she suddenly dinna have the need to run. Alex. He'd erased any doubt of where she belonged and who she belonged to. No wonder the church warned of the careless giving and taking of flesh. Something so special, so sacred, should be reserved for a husband and wife. That's what she'd learned in her short time of intimacy with her husband.

But did he feel the same?

Could he feel anything after living as a heathen, beyond the grace of God?

"Keely?" Alex sat up. "Are ye all right, lass?"

"Aye."

"Come back to bed then."

"I am hungry." Her stomach growled.

Alex grinned. "Our bedsport has given ye a better appetite."

Keely wandered to the table and picked over the bread, cheese, and meat. Anything would taste good right now. She chewed a piece of smoked venison and swallowed it down with a sip of wine. "Are ye hungry?" She gazed at Alex.

"In a different way, lass." The same expression that had darkened his face earlier was back. The look of lust.

She would never forget—even if she tried. No man had ever looked at her like that.

He threw the furs back.

Keely couldna keep her eyes off him as he stood up. His blond hair hung lose about his shoulders. And his powerful body, all that muscle and tanned skin, his confident stride ... his erection. She closed her eyes for a quick moment and sucked in a breath. Aye, his member was long and thick and ready to be inside her again. He dinna need food or drink, he wanted her. As he reached her, he caressed her cheek, and she shivered.

"What will it take to coax ye back to bed?" he asked.

She pretended to think on it. "Something special, I think."

"How special?"

She looked down. "*Very* special."

Alex chuckled. "Kiss me, Keely."

A foot taller than her, she stood on her toes and locked her hands behind his neck, pulling him down. Something sparked between them as their lips met, and Keely felt the wetness between her legs again.

"Is it always this easy between a man and woman, Alex?"

"Nay," he said. "We share something rare. And I canna get enough of ye." He dragged her from the table over to the closest chair and sat down. He patted his lap. "Straddle me."

"How?"

"Very slowly, I doona wish to hurt ye." Guiding her, he sunk inside her as she lowered herself on top of him.

It felt so different. Though she was overly sensitive between her legs, no pain ensued. Instinctively, she started to roll her hips while Alex held on.

"That's it, lass. Doona stop."

She'd never thought it possible that a woman could take control. She liked it, perhaps more than she should. But just as she was getting familiar with how to move, Alex lifted her and carried her to the wall. He pressed her back against the cold, smooth stones, holding her up while he thrust inside her. Was there no end to the pleasure? No end to how many ways her new husband could bed her?

Alex stopped moving and bit his lower lip. "I canna hold it, lass. I am sorry for it."

She dinna care, he'd already given her so much enjoyment, so much hope.

Once he stopped convulsing, he lifted her chin and placed a kiss on her lips. "We should sleep now."

They walked hand-in-hand back to the bed. As she slipped under the furs, Keely couldna remember a time when she felt so content. Alex turned on his side and pulled her close, keeping an arm around her. "Sleep well, milady," he whispered.

She smiled as she closed her eyes, hoping her dreams were as sweet as the memories she'd made with her husband that night.

Chapter Fifteen

DESPITE THE TEMPTATION to stay with his wife, Alex knew there was much work to be done. He was careful not to make too much noise as he slipped out of the bed to find his clothes. Aye—the night couldna have gone better. Keely was everything a man could want in bed. Her scent lingered all over him, and he liked it that way. He washed his face and hands, then dressed. Once his boots were on, he walked to the door and knocked four times.

The bolt slid back and one of the guards opened it for him. "Good morn, Laird Alex," Iain said with a stupid smile.

Alex nodded and stepped into the corridor. "Let my wife sleep. When she is ready, she is free to walk about the keep and bailey. But one of ye must stay with her at all times."

"Aye," Iain said.

Alex made his way belowstairs, and was welcomed by the council and his captains.

"Food," he demanded, claiming his seat at the high table.

A maid set a trencher of warm oats in front of him, then filled his cup with ale.

"Ye survived the long night. Did ye bring the sheet?" Mathe asked.

"What sheet?" Alex swallowed his first bite of food.

"The bloody sheet from yer bridal bed," Mathe explained.

"To provide the necessary evidence of yer wife's purity. There's been much talk of it."

"And who is entitled to see it?"

"The council, your captains, and perhaps any clan member who is interested. This marriage isna a private affair, milord. Hundreds of people are depending on ye, on Lady MacKay, to set things right, to heal the wounds so cruelly inflicted by the past and the Sutherlands. In short, Alex, hope."

"And a blasted sheet will give ye that hope?" He couldna understand why any of them would doubt his ability to determine whether his young bride was an innocent or not. "My word should suffice. I did see virgin's blood."

Mathe leaned closer and spoke quietly. "I believe ye."

"Let that be enough."

"Nay."

"What do ye mean, nay?"

"There are those like Angus. Tenants filled with superstitions who need to see the physical evidence to satisfy their doubts. The sheet should be hung from the window in yer bedchamber or even here in the great hall."

Alex growled with disapproval. "I dinna bed my wife in the usual way."

Mathe raised a brow. "Milord?"

Alex sighed and scrubbed his face. Did he really need to explain? Perhaps. The older man clung to tradition like the superstitious crofters he spoke about. "We dinna use the bed, Mathe. Not the first time."

The councilman's mouth opened, but nothing came out.

"Are ye going to call me a heathen again?"

"I doona know what to say, Alexander. Is Lady Keely well?"

"Sleeping as sound as a babe."

"Something must be done, milord. Quickly."

With the sudden loss of his appetite, Alex shot up from his chair and rushed upstairs. Instead of returning to the laird's bedchamber where Keely slept, he went to her room. Fresh linens were folded and kept on a shelf near the bed. He selected a sheet, opened it, and then used the dirk from his boot to cut himself on the wrist. Very carefully, he sprinkled a fair amount of blood on the material. "There's yer virgin's blood," he said out loud.

He left the soiled linen on the bed and went back to the great hall to find a maid.

Fortunately, Leah was available. "Go to my wife's chamber and bring the bridal sheet belowstairs. Present it to Captain Mathe and do with it as he asks."

Leah curtsied and left.

Alex once again claimed his chair at the high table. "Leah will fetch the sheet ye asked for."

"Good," Mathe said. "Are ye happy, Alex? Will Keely suit?"

Alex took a drink of ale. "She'll suit."

He finished his meal in silence, then motioned for his captains to follow him outside. The west village must be rebuilt. If it wasn't, the Sutherlands would see it as a sign of fear. And he'd be damned if the earl would be given any opportunity to claim victory over the MacKays.

A squire saddled his horse and brought him out of the stable. Alex mounted, waiting for the rest of his men to do the same. The west village was a short ride away. Since he hadn't taken the time to tour it after the battle, it was a long overdue visit.

An hour later, they approached the outskirts. It dinna take long for Alex to see the devastation, burned out huts and scorched earth. The gardens were even destroyed. Nothing had been spared. It enraged Alex that such violence was directed at his people, instead of at him or the MacKay soldiers. Women and children had died or been kidnapped.

"There is nothing worth saving." Jamie rode up beside him.

"Except for our pride."

"Aye," his cousin reluctantly agreed. "There is that."

"What it's worth," Alex added.

"Not much to a Sutherland."

"But everything to a MacKay," Alex finished.

Nearly a hundred people had lived there. Though one of the smaller villages, the tenants were hard workers and produced the finest wool and tastiest vegetables for his table. It had always been that way. As a child, Alex would play with the children who lived there, spending hours swimming in the nearby loch and eating supper with whatever family invited him to stay.

He dismounted and walked to a random spot where a hut once stood. He crouched and picked up a clump of earth and smelled it, rich soil—the best his lands had to offer.

"How many huts were here?" he asked.

"Seventeen," one of his men answered.

"Rebuild every one of them, better than before. I want a defensive wall constructed as well—four feet high, from stone."

"Alex." Jamie joined him. "The time and expense..."

"No expense will be spared, Jamie. Remember, with my new lairdship comes my well-supplied purse. The MacKays willna go without again."

"And what will happen the next time a Sutherland decides to attack the village?"

"We will be prepared. A guardhouse is to be built as well. Four soldiers will be permanently stationed here."

His cousin nodded, but Alex knew he disagreed with his choices.

Alex wouldna let the land stand fallow. Nay, he'd use the strategies he'd learned while he was away and make the

MacKays a feared clan. Even the keep required updating. He wanted to construct a new tower and reinforce the outer wall. They also needed to recruit new soldiers. All of it would be financed by his own gold and silver.

"Where do ye wish to go next?" Jamie asked.

"We will visit all of the westward villages today. Leave half of the men here to start working, the rest will come with us."

Jamie immediately departed to make sure his orders were followed.

The earl would pay for his treachery even though there was no direct proof linking the man to this violence. Spilled blood required revenge. An eye for an eye—as the Almighty demanded. Alex wouldna rest until the debt was paid in full.

KEELY KNEW SHE had to brave going belowstairs. As Lady MacKay, earning the respect and trust of the clan meant everything to her. She couldna hide in her bedchamber forever. With Leah at her side, she descended the stairs, hoping to be welcomed by someone.

The colorful tapestry and weapons hanging over the main hearth in the great hall had been covered with a blood-stained sheet. Keely couldna believe her eyes. And though she understood the importance of the symbol, it was a lie.

"Milady," Leah urged her mistress onward. "Ye must take yer seat at the high table."

"That dinna come from our bridal bed," she informed Leah.

"Aye. Laird Alex sent me to retrieve it from yer bedchamber."

"But why?"

Her every move was being carefully watched by the soldiers

and servants in the hall. It was bad enough she'd woken in an empty bed, learning from her maid that Alex had ridden off with his captains. But to have to stare at the sheet while she broke her fast… It dinna set right with her.

"Remove the unseemly thing," she commanded Leah.

The maid hesitated, looking about the hall before she finally nodded and searched for a chair to stand on so she could reach it. Leah dragged the heavy piece of furniture as close to the hearth as she could get it, then climbed up. Just as she started to reach for the end of the sheet, Mathe approached.

"Nay," he called out. "Climb down, Mistress Leah."

"But sir…" the maid said.

"Doona stop, Leah," Keely instructed her.

"Lady Keely," Mathe said. "The sheet must stay."

"I disagree, Captain Mathe. After all…" she whispered. "Tis my blood on it, is it not?"

The captain's cheeks turned scarlet. "If ye'd come with me." He took her arm, gently encouraging her to walk with him. "A conversation better held in private."

Keely stopped walking. "And where would we find a place to talk alone?"

"Yer husband's solar, perhaps?"

Keely shook her head. "And give the clan something else to wag their tongues over? I am well aware that my reputation is questionable, Captain Mathe, but I wouldna want to give the maids a reason to start talking ill of ye. Anything ye have to say will be spoken here."

"Christ's blood," the normally mild captain exclaimed as he huffed out a breath. "I dinna think I'd live to see the day when the Almighty would deliver a woman with a tongue as careless as her laird's."

Keely couldna hold back the morbid laugh. "What are ye

trying to say?"

"Lady Keely..." He cleared his throat. "That sheet is to remain hanging in the hall for ten days—enough time for any MacKay or visitor to satisfy their moral curiosity."

"Moral curiosity? Just what is that, sir?"

"Proof of yer innocence."

Keely bit her tongue. What she was dying to say included something about how indecent her wedding night with her new husband had been—how there'd been no sheet to capture her virgin blood. Aye, perhaps she had spent too much time around Alex in the past—and six older brothers who rarely refrained from expressing themselves in front of her. "Ye require evidence of my innocence, Captain Mathe, but the very thing used to prove it is vulgar in every way!"

"'Tis not abhorrent in any way, Lady Keely."

"Nay? Shall I tell ye what it made me think of the moment I saw it?"

Mathe tugged at his collar. "I-I believe I can guess without further explanation."

"May I be of some help?" Petro appeared suddenly.

Keely gazed at the scholar. Where had he come from? Did it matter? She more than appreciated his presence. "Good morn," she greeted him, trying to banish her sour mood.

"Good morn," he returned with a smile. "Perhaps Captain Mathe would prefer finishing his ale. Laird Alex asked me to keep an eye out for you. Unfortunately, he needed to inspect the west village so he could make the necessary arrangements to rebuild the place. A walk would be nice." He offered his arm.

Keely dinna need to think about it, she accepted. "Please send Leah out," she told the captain.

Mathe bowed his head out of duty, nothing more. "As ye wish." He rushed back to the hall.

"I have waited for this moment," Petro said.

"My moment of utter shame?"

He chuckled. "No. The pleasure of your company, milady, a chance to speak alone."

"I doona see why. I am sure ye've been exposed to the gossip."

"I am a man of science, Lady Keely. If I listened to every rumor, then the process of discovery would be wasted on me. I prefer to gather facts, then make my own judgments."

In that moment, Keely decided she liked Petro, immensely. "Then tell me what ye wish to know."

Leah joined them. "Shall I retrieve our walking cloaks?"

"Aye," Keely said. "We will be in the bailey, Leah."

The fresh air immediately restored Keely's calm. The sun peeked out from behind wispy, white clouds, and the fragrant breeze cooled her cheeks. "Some would say this mild weather is a good omen of things to come in my marriage."

"Others would suggest it might be the calm before the storm."

There was no malice on the scholar's face. Nay, the man simply appreciated quick wit and probably found he dinna get much here. Not that the MacKays were lacking in education. Alex and his brother were well tutored as lads. Alex could read and write, as could several of his captains. It's what they read that worried her the most. Closed minds—superstitious tenants—a strong belief in God but fear of the tiny creatures that were believed to haunt the mountains and lochs.

"Our fate was sealed long ago," she repeated Alex's own words. "So no signs from heaven can change our future, I'm afraid."

"Ah," he said. "But you can."

They strolled past soldiers practicing maneuvers and younger recruits shooting arrows at grass-stuffed targets. Children were playing while some of the women were busy washing clothes and sorting vegetables from the gardens. The wedding celebration hadn't changed the reality of the next day. If it had been a normal wedding, the celebration would have lasted for days, maybe even a week.

"Aye, if I had supporters among the MacKays."

"Do you not?"

Keely thought about it. "Leah."

"Did you forget me? Or the Kalil brothers?"

She hadn't considered them. "Five out of several thousand—tis not much."

"It's a start, milady."

Leah finally appeared with their light, wool cloaks and one of the guards assigned to stay with Keely. She pinned her cloak in place, then quickly started to walk with Petro again.

"What has my husband told ye about me?"

"Many things." His eyes sparkled in the sunlight.

"I know ye travelled together from Italy."

The scholar nodded. "I met Alex a few months after he left here."

"Was he…" she hesitated.

"Angry?"

"Aye."

"I've never met a more miserable man."

Some women might like hearing it, but Keely dinna. Though she did possess a certain amount of curiosity about his past, the guilt still hung heavy about her neck like a millstone.

The guards opened the main gates for them, and Petro ushered her through, Leah and her armed escort keeping a respectable distance behind them. The fact that she had any freedom to come and go pleased Keely. For if he'd wanted to,

Alex could have locked her abovestairs.

They followed a well-worn path to the loch where so much of Keely's finest memories with the MacKays had happened. Fishing and swimming, lazy afternoons spent with Alex and John, and a host of tenants she'd always considered friends.

"This land is different than my home," Petro observed.

"In what way? I've always wondered about Italy."

"Tis a sensuous place."

Keely liked the way he described his home. "I've never heard a man describe his land like that."

"Rome is a crowded city—filled with saints and sinners."

"The Highlands have few of their own."

His smile reached his dark eyes. "And I think you consider your husband one of those sinners."

She shrugged. "I am a woman, sir. My opinion means little."

"It means something to me."

"Why?"

"I will tell you what I told Alex. I pledged loyalty to your husband, and will serve him faithfully. But that doesn't mean I cannot be your friend, Lady Keely. Whatever you confide in me will stay between us. Unless it threatens the life of Alex—that is where I draw the line of distinction."

"I accept yer offer of friendship, then."

"Good."

They reached the loch and Keely went to her favorite boulder. She kicked her shoes off and raised her gown just enough so she could dip her toes in the water.

"Another thing I like about Scotland."

"Oh?"

"Your desire to experience the world around you. In Italy, a noble woman would not be caught in the water."

"There are people nearby that would frown on my actions,

sir."

"Perhaps a Sutherland?"

"Always a Sutherland."

"The same with the sheet in the great hall?"

Were all of his conversations so circular, so connected? The man had a talent for disarming her, getting her to say things she'd usually keep to herself—as smooth talking as a poet, and as entertaining as an actor. "A barbaric practice."

"Highlanders *are* barbarians."

That surprised Keely. "How so, sir?"

"What do you think gave Alex the ability to thrive in Constantinople? Sure, his pale skin and hair already set him apart from most—but he adapted quickly—understood the ancient ways of the people. That's a rare talent. And the nobles of that great place recognized his value, as did I the moment we met."

"I canna deny the lack of refinement here. We are far away from the king's court and the elegant cities of Europe. But what we lack in manners, we make up for in morals. The Scots are a noble people, ruled by God and honor."

"You are a fine match for Alexander," he said. "A worthy lady."

"Now, if only my husband agreed with ye."

"Do not let him forget it. Be everything he thinks you are not."

She frowned and gazed at Petro. "That willna take much."

Petro chuckled. "Only the good things."

"Do ye have a wife?"

The expression on Petro's face changed as he stared across the water into some distant time and place. "A long time ago. I was married at fifteen."

"So young."

"Yes."

"What happened?"

"Plague." He visibly shivered. "My wife and son were taken from me too soon." He looked back at her, forcing another smile. "Even Alex does not know that part of my history."

"I am sorry for yer great loss." Words couldna express how sad Keely felt for her new friend. And though Petro seemed to manage his suffering, the pain in his eyes showed, whether he knew it or not. "How is it that Alex doesna know?"

"Alexander carried his own grief, Lady Keely. I refused to add to that burden."

"B-but Alex would want to know."

"Maybe someday—when he finally decides what kind of man he wants to be."

"Tell me of yer wife and son…"

"Anuria and Giuseppe were everything to me. What does a boy of that age know, really? I went from my father's house to the cottage gifted to us on our wedding day. It was a quiet life, spent together. As the younger children of nobles, we were not expected to toil in the fields, only to produce grandchildren that would keep our family names alive for another generation. But that unholy sickness claimed thousands in Rome that year—no house, no family was left untouched."

Keely reached for his hand. Petro squeezed her fingers in appreciation.

"We are blessed in the north here," she said. "The plague has never ripped our children from our arms. But war has many times."

Petro nodded in acknowledgement. "At least you have a chance to see and fight your adversaries. Sickness is an invisible evil that no man can defeat. Only luck and the grace of God can save you from its clutches."

She let go of his hand. "Have ye ever swam in a Scottish

loch?"

"Never," he said.

"Let us change that." She unpinned her cloak and gestured for Leah to join them. "For I have never known the waters to fail to put a smile on my face."

Petro watched her strip down to her shift, then waited for Leah to do the same. "Is it cold?" he asked.

"Aye,' Keely said, braving the water first. She waded out to where it reached her hips. "Leah. Petro. Come!"

The scholar waved at her, then slowly unlaced his boots, removed his tunic, and took Leah's hand, both of them laughing as they splashed out into the loch.

Aye, Keely thought, this was her favorite place on MacKay lands. And if she concentrated hard enough, the echo of her and Alex's laughter from long ago rang in her ears. That was the magic of the Highlands, a place that never let her forget who and what she was, the same place that Petro had decided to give up his own beloved home for—a place she'd never trade for anything, even freedom.

Chapter Sixteen

After spending a long day inspecting the west villages, Alex and his men returned to the keep, hungry and in need of sleep. Expecting his wife to greet him in the hall, he was displeased to find Mathe instead.

Alex dinna want to hear the old captain's complaints. But the faster he walked, the louder the captain pressed him for immediate attention.

"Laird Alex, if I may have a moment of yer time."

"I am not in the mood to discuss anything."

"It is urgent."

Alex spun about. "The only matter of importance is guaranteeing my people the Sutherlands willna be able to destroy their homes again."

"Aye," Mathe said respectfully. "But ye asked me to stay behind to protect this household."

Alex gazed around the hall. "The walls are still standing. Ye have my gratitude."

"Tis yer wife."

Three words Alex had hoped not to hear. "Did she try to run away?"

"Nay."

Inside, Alex felt relieved. "What is it, then?"

"She doesna want the bridal bed sheet to be left hanging."

Alex eyed the linen. "Do ye blame the lass?"

Mathe sputtered a bit, but collected himself enough to continue. "It is a matter of tradition. And under the circumstances, it is more important than ever that no one is given a chance to question the legitimacy of yer union."

Alex pursed his lips. He'd be the judge of his wife's chastity, not the council and surely not his tenants. "As I've explained to ye before, Captain Mathe, I am capable of vouching for my wife's purity."

"Please," Mathe pleaded. "Doona take it down."

Alex rubbed his dry, burning eyes. The wind had kicked up enough dust to blind a man. "Are ye the one who needs convincing, Mathe?"

"Are ye questioning my support, Laird Alex? Am I not the one who demanded ye stay? Marry? Accept responsibility for the clan?"

Aye—the man was right. "Where is Lady Keely?"

"Abovestairs."

"I will speak with her. The linen stays. Now, can I eat and drink, perhaps spend another night with my bride without worrying about domestic issues?"

"I will have a maid bring yer supper up."

Alex chuckled. "Perhaps my brother chose the wrong head of household."

Mathe dinna take his observation as a compliment. "I believe one of the younger retainers would be better suited for the duty."

"Aye. Select the man and return to training in the morn. There is much to be done, Mathe."

The captain bowed and departed for the kitchens.

Alex dragged himself abovestairs, immediately dismissing the guards standing at his bedchamber door. "I doona need ye tonight."

He stepped inside, finding his wife curled up on one of the chairs in front of the hearth. She dinna acknowledge his presence, but Alex knew she wasna asleep. "Did ye enjoy yer first day as mistress of this keep?"

Her agitated sigh gave him the answer he sought.

"It will take time."

"It will take a miracle," she shot back, sitting up. "Why did ye provide that bloody linen for Mathe?"

"To keep peace."

"Yer efforts are wasted on that man."

Alex swallowed his temper as he sat on the end of the bed and started to unlace his boots. Patience was in short supply today. "Captain Mathe is a loyal servant and skilled warrior. My grandfather appointed him as his own squire and my sire made him a captain. And he dinna like what happened between ye and John. Ye must give everyone time to adjust to the idea of ye being here, Keely." He dropped his second boot on the floor.

"I dinna want to stay."

Alex growled. "Choose yer words more wisely."

"Perhaps ye should follow yer own advice, Husband."

"And what do ye mean by that?"

He stood.

"Ye should have used better judgment in choosing a wife."

Alex rubbed his chin. The she-devil had a sharp tongue that he might never be able to change. "I chose well."

"Did ye?" She hugged her center, not looking like she believed him. "I like Petro."

The change in subject eased the tension between his shoulder blades. "Aye?"

"Aye," she confirmed. "He has a talent for showing up when trouble is building."

Alex smiled. "That he does."

"Mathe and I were having words and he immediately offered his assistance."

"And what kind of solution did he propose?"

"A walk."

"And where did ye take him?"

"To the loch for a swim."

"What?"

"Aye. With Leah and our guard."

The picture in his mind made him feel uneasy—the idea of his wife stripping down in front of another man. Even on the hottest of days, the water was cold, and Alex knew her nipples would poke right through the thin material of her shift. The most honorable of men would have a difficult time not sneaking a peek at her lush breasts. But he kept his jealousy to himself. "I dinna know Petro could swim."

"If ye consider sinking like a stone swimming."

"But he dinna drown?"

"Nay. I am sure he is sleeping like a babe."

Alex chuckled. "He dinna give up easily?"

"I doona believe the man knows the meaning. I spent hours teaching him how to float, kick his feet, and move his arms."

"Did ye succeed?"

"Aye."

"Then I am happy for ye, Keely. Yer day was more productive than my own."

Concern etched her face as she came to him. "What is it, Alex?"

"The west villages are very vulnerable to Sutherland attacks."

"Isna everyone vulnerable?"

"Aye. The earl grows more powerful by the year. His alliances in England are strong."

"What will ye do?"

Alex sat back down and closed his eyes, too weary to hide his emotions. "I would kill John de Moravia and put an end to this conflict forever."

Keely knelt in front of him, resting her hand on his knee. "With three sons…"

"Aye. The torch of war would simply be passed to the next earl."

"Have ye considered an alliance through marriage?"

"It would be hard to accept for yer father, the Gunns, Sinclairs, and MacLeods. And I have no heir." He gazed at his wife. "If we are blessed with a son, would Helen Sutherland be willing to wait so many years to take a husband, one young enough to be her own son?"

"There is Jamie, and the earl has six nieces, three without husbands."

"Nay." Alex couldna do it. "I willna condemn my cousin to such a marriage."

"But the earl's nieces are lovely."

"They are Sutherlands." He caressed her cheek. "Yer council is valuable, Keely."

"Thank ye," she said sweetly.

The time for discussing clan affairs with his wife was over. Alex wanted to focus on other things. "How are ye feeling?" He'd been less than gentle with her last eve—years of desire slowly sated by every deep thrust into her body. As he stared into her eyes, that desire began to brim over again. It would take three lifetimes to satisfy his hunger where Keely MacKay was concerned. Damn his soul for it. Damn her for being so irresistible.

"I am well, milord."

"Nay soreness?"

"Only a little."

"Tis expected."

"Leah had me soak in a hot bath with soothing herbs."

"If ye need to rest..."

"I doona," she cut him off.

"Then ye enjoyed our lovemaking?"

"Aye."

"Ye are magnificent, Keely." He pulled her to her feet.

More than willing to be touched, Alex cupped her breasts through her gown. They were bountiful enough to spill over the sides of his hands, but not overly large. He couldna rest without tasting her again. Working the laces on her bodice quickly, he released her tender flesh and suckled a nipple while he slipped his hand beneath her skirts, finding her wetness. The faster he stroked, the louder she moaned. The little noises pleased him, made his cock ache for relief.

His arms and legs wrapped around her, bringing her down on top of him on the mattress. Their foreheads touched and he kissed her, exploring the depths of her sweet mouth. Keely managed to hike her skirts above her waist, exposing herself completely. Alex reached for her arse, guiding her upward, her mound mere inches from his mouth. Christ, he wished he could control himself better, but a man shouldna deprive himself of what he needed. And for Alex, his young wife was as necessary as the air he breathed.

"What are ye doing, Alex?" She eyed him warily.

"Doona be nervous."

"There is nowhere left for me to comfortably sit. So why are ye pulling me up to your..."

His tongue provided the answer. Her luscious backside filled his palms as he silently instructed her on how to move across his face. Finding her center, he sucked mercilessly as she lost control—throwing her head back and riding him wildly.

"Aye, Keely," he breathed. "This is what I've longed for, to make ye mine over and over again."

Moments later… "A-Alex." Her body trembled from the intensity of the release.

Proud of what little effort it took to satisfy her, Alex rearranged his wife in the middle of the bed. She spread her legs and held onto his biceps. "More," she said.

"More of what, ye wanton?"

"Ye."

He sheathed himself deep inside her, and they moved together, their union more familiar, more relaxed. Alex flicked his tongue over her nipples, then claimed her mouth until the need to fill her with his seed overwhelmed him. He arched his back, and Keely locked her hands behind his neck, writhing underneath him.

No words could describe how she made him feel or what she stole from him every time he came. It wasna as easy as he thought to safeguard his heart from her. Nay. Keely had a wicked way about her, intentional or not. And if he dinna be careful, she'd own more than his body.

Exhausted, he rolled onto his back, playing with a strand of her dark hair. "Do ye wish to finish our conversation from earlier?"

"Which part?"

"The sheet."

"Ye're determined to placate Mathe. My feelings are secondary, Alex. I may not agree with it, but I understand."

"Do ye, or are ye just saying that to keep the peace between us?" He looked at her.

"Peace is in short supply here. Anything I can do to help, I will."

Once again, her words pleased him. His original plan had been to give her a taste of the pain she'd caused him. He raised his right arm, resting the back of his hand against his forehead. Whatever was happening to him, the need to hurt her was fading. She was right, peace was in short supply. The less strife at home the better. It would allow him to focus on the improvements needed to defend his people and lands.

Someone knocked on the door, and Alex growled. He'd forgotten about the tray Mathe had promised to send up. Not ashamed of his nakedness, he crawled out of bed and strutted to the door. He opened it and took the tray from the maid.

"Are ye hungry?" he asked, walking to the table, his stomach rumbling from the smell of fresh meat and bread.

Keely sat up. "Is there enough for both of us?"

Alex lifted the linen covering the food. "Aye."

She joined him at the table, fidgeting with her bodice.

"Nay." He reached for her hand. "Nothing would please me more than filling my belly and having the pleasure of gazing upon your breasts at the same time."

She smiled and sat on the chair across from him. "As ye wish, milord."

He served her some meat and bread, then poured them each a cup of wine. As he ate his fill, Alex wondered if in time he could learn to trust, maybe even love Keely again.

Chapter Seventeen

A WEEK LATER, Mathe and several other guards rushed inside the great hall where Alex and Keely had just sat down at the high table. "What is all the commotion about?" Alex asked.

"Milord," Mathe bowed. "Laird Oliphant is here."

"My father?" Keely shot up from her chair.

"Nay." Alex prevented her escape. "Sit down, Keely. Please."

"But. Alex... I havena seen my sire for years. Do ye not approve of a reunion?"

"Alexander MacKay!"

Alex couldna ever forget that booming voice. Obviously, the laird had forced his way through the bailey, for Alex hadn't invited anyone inside.

"What will ye have me do?" Mathe asked.

"Who is with Laird Oliphant?"

"Thirty soldiers and four of his sons."

"God's bones," Alex cursed.

He dinna have a chance to say anything else, for Laird Oliphant stormed the great hall with his progeny in tow.

Though Keely obeyed him and stayed on the dais, she stood immediately. "Father?"

"Keely?" Laird Oliphant strode across the room. "Alexander, what is this I hear? Ye wed my only daughter without my blessing?"

"I welcome ye, Laird Oliphant, or should I call ye Father now?" Alex walked around the table, his fingers resting loosely on the hilt of his sword.

Matthew Oliphant was an imposing man. His snow-white beard and hair dinna mean a bloody thing. He was as strong as a bull, a fearless fighter, and rightfully angry. Alex hoped their first meeting wouldna end with violence.

"That depends on what my daughter has to say. Keely, why are ye standing there, lass? Come down here at once!"

She eyed her sire, visibly shaken, then looked to Alex. If he forbade her from going to her da, it would hurt her in a way he couldna fix. It dinna matter, she rushed off the dais and into her sire's arms. Laird Oliphant embraced her, then held her at arm's length, studying her face.

"Lass," he said gently. "Ye broke my heart."

"I am sorry, Father."

"Where have ye been?"

"That is a matter better discussed in my solar," Alex interjected.

Not letting go of his daughter, Laird Oliphant threw Alex a dark look. "Truth is better told in the open. And if the rumors that reached my ears are true, I will have yer head, MacKay, and a good measure of yer blood, too."

"Nay." Keely took her father's hand. "And Broc and Gavin," she addressed two of her brothers, who were eager to pull their weapons. "Stand down, please."

Mathe and several of the MacKay guards surged forward, forming a semicircle around Keely's family.

"Violence willna change anything. I am legally wed to Laird Alex. The proof is hanging over the hearth." She gestured at the very thing she despised, the blood-stained sheet.

"That means nothing," her sire growled, the evidence of their wedding night only deepening his resentment. "It redeems ye, but not him." He pointed at Alex. "She took vows with yer brother, John."

Alex ignored the insult. Arguing with a man blinded by rage would accomplish nothing but getting one of them killed. There'd been enough bloodshed lately. And Alex owed his father-in-law a generous measure of tolerance. If Keely were his daughter, he would demand justice, too. "If ye will come with me, Laird Oliphant, my secretary will show ye the legal documents that will prove her union with John was invalid. I mean no disrespect to ye or yer sons."

"Keely." Her father gave her a gentle shake. "Tell me where ye've been all this time? The missives I received revealed little and were delivered by men unwilling to say a word. Did ye flee this place and go to the convent? What was the purpose of all the secrecy? Did John hurt ye?"

"No, Father. I will answer yer questions, but not here."

Laird Oliphant nodded, letting her go. "Laird John died not a sennight ago and ye're already remarried?"

"Matthew," Alex gritted out. "There are things ye doona understand." If the man only knew how close Alex was to losing his temper. "Will ye join us in my solar?"

"Broc will come, too." Laird Oliphant waved at his eldest son. "The rest of ye, stay here."

Breathing a sigh of relief, Alex led the way. Keely shared a worried look with him as he opened the door and invited her father to cross the threshold first. Thankfully, the chamber had high ceilings and plenty of room, for Alex needed some space. Petro rose from his chair behind the desk and bowed as Alex walked in and closed the door.

"This is my interpreter and secretary, Petro de' Medici."

Laird Oliphant bent his head in recognition. "Get on with it, Alexander."

Keely and her brother sat down in the chairs along the back wall while her father and Alex claimed the padded seats at the desk.

"Laird Oliphant, Keely's sire, wishes to know why I married his daughter," Alex told Petro.

Petro immediately shuffled through the ledgers and papers on the desk. "If you will take the time to read these letters, I am sure you will find the information you seek."

"Missives? From who?"

"From my father and brother," Alex clarified. "And one from Father Michael."

"I'm not interested in the words of dead men," Matthew spat. "Speak plainly, Alex. There are no soldiers to keep us from shedding each other's blood in here."

"Nay, there are not," he agreed. "Are ye prepared for the truth, sir?"

"I am prepared to listen."

Alex stood and started to pace. He'd prefer to speak one-on-one with his father-in-law. But as he scanned the faces of his wife, Broc, and Petro, he agreed they all deserved to witness the conversation. The future hung in the balance. "Before ye commanded yer daughter to marry John, we were handfasted."

Laird Oliphant stretched his long legs out and dinna speak.

"Something my father claimed ye were aware of."

"If I may, Alex," Petro said. "Consent was given in the form of sacred vows spoken between your daughter and Alex. According to canon law and the law in Scotland, consent supersedes any betrothal or marriage made thereafter."

"Holy Christ!" Laird Oliphant fisted his hands. "This wasna supposed to happen."

"Father," Keely said. "I did as ye asked and married John."

Her father twisted round in his chair, staring at her. "Yer virgin blood is on that sheet, Keely. How could ye have married Laird John?"

"We dinna consummate the marriage."

"And why not, girl?"

Keely averted her gaze.

"She ran away," Alex answered for her.

"Why?" her father pressed.

Broc took her by the hand. "Be brave, lass. Tell our sire whatever he wishes to know."

"I-It's not that easy, Broc." She palmed tears from her eyes.

"Why the hell not?" her father blasted.

Keely's lips quivered, and Alex wished he could help her, save her from this inquisition. But truth be told, she needed to learn to stand up to her sire the same way she challenged him and his captains. The lass had it inside her, she just needed to find the courage.

"I dinna love John."

"Love?" her sire scoffed. "If love had anything to do with marriage, the Highlands would be long gone."

"I doona understand, Father."

"Matches are made to benefit the future of our clans, not to sate the passion in yer heart. Alex was but a whelp. It was John who held the future of Clan MacKay in his hands."

"John is dead," she observed.

"Aye—put in an early grave by ye and his only brother."

"Enough!" Alex slammed his fist on the table, startling Keely and her father. "John was killed defending our lands from Sutherlands."

"His death is convenient for ye, too, is it not?" Matthew accused. "For look at ye now, *Laird MacKay*."

"Father…" Broc stood.

"Sit down, lad. I'll have my say."

"At what cost?" Alex asked.

"She is *my* child."

"Keely is *my* wife."

Silence swallowed the room.

"Does my happiness mean nothing to ye?" Keely asked.

"Where did ye run to, Keely?" Broc asked.

"Dunrobin Castle," she said.

"Jesus Christ," Broc growled. "Ye chose the Sutherlands over us? Over John? Over anyone else? I canna stand being in the same room with ye!"

Broc slapped Keely's face hard enough for her to cry out. Not from pain, Alex knew, but from the shock of it. Broc wasna a violent man.

Alex kicked his chair aside and rushed Broc.

Keely shielded her brother, standing between Alex and him. "Nay, Alex. I willna let ye retaliate. I deserved it."

"No one has the right to strike ye, Keely."

"Nay? I'd rather be kicked in the gut than have ye all tugging me in different directions." She covered her face with both hands, then let out a strangled sound. Squaring her shoulders, she looked between her husband and father. "I doona wish to witness any more hatred." She stormed out of the solar and slammed the door.

Laird Oliphant was the first to speak. "She has always been a biddable lass."

Alex laughed bitterly. "Ye doona know yer daughter very well, sir. For she's anything but obedient, and I wouldna wish her to be anything else."

KEELY RAN DOWN the stairs, then marched through the great hall. She'd meant every word she had said to Alex and her sire. When would they consider her feelings?

"Lady Keely," Mathe called, following her outside.

"I doona wish to speak to ye, Mathe."

"Ye're not allowed to wander about without an escort."

She clenched her hands. "Get behind me, devil," she swore. "I have reached my limit, Captain. I will walk alone, and if ye send anyone after me, I will punch him in the nose."

Mathe gaped at her for a brief moment, then bowed. "Aye, milady."

Satisfied he had taken her seriously, Keely headed for the loch. She perched on one of the boulders, admiring the water. Happier times had been known there. She and Alex dinna have to worry about anything. And they'd fallen in love so easily.

Her solitude dinna last; she heard the crunch of grass and gravel beneath someone's boots.

"Lady Keely?"

It was Petro.

"Did Alex send ye?" If he had, she'd send the scholar back to him.

"No. I excused myself and decided to find you."

"I am glad," she admitted. "Ye're the only person I could tolerate right now."

"And how did I win such favor?"

She gestured for him to sit on the rock next to her. "By not making any demands of me and by treating me as an equal."

He sat down. "I've always found women more intelligent than men."

"Aye?"

"Why else would God bless you with the ability to carry children and give birth?"

"I think most women have been taught it's a curse, punishment for Eve's sins."

Petro chuckled. "Men wrote the holy book, Lady Keely. And men are the ones to teach it. How different it might be if women were entrusted with such things."

She stared at him in shock. "Have ye shared these thoughts with anyone else?"

"Never."

"Good," she said. "I think ye better not. If Father Michael overheard ye, he might have ye burned at the stake."

"Which only proves my point."

"So it does," she agreed.

"Do you mind if I ask you a question?"

"Nay."

"Why did ye run to the Sutherlands?" he asked.

"I will not apologize for my choice."

"I do not expect you to."

"I couldna face my sire. By leaving John, I betrayed the MacKays and my family. I sought refuge in the one place I knew no one would look for me. Though I never intended to stay there for five years."

"And Earl Sutherland was only too happy to oblige."

"I was made welcome from the moment his men discovered me."

"Alex has mentioned the earl's youngest son, a bastard, I believe."

"Struan."

"You spent time with him?"

"Aye."

"Did he ever make demands of you?"

Keely dinna understand. "Demands?"

"Did he show ye affection? Ask you to marry him?"

"'Twas mentioned on occasion. Not only by Struan, but the earl, too. An impossibility, for at the time, I believed myself married to Laird John. Why do ye ask?"

Petro reached inside his tunic and produced a missive with a broken wax seal. Keely immediately recognized the Sutherland crest and her heart plummeted.

"I am able to act on Laird Alex's behalf concerning all forms of business. I intercepted this missive yesterday. It is from the earl, expressing his displeasure of your marriage to Alex. He claims you for his youngest son."

"I-I…" she stumbled on her words, rendered speechless by the news.

"Worry not," he assured her. "Your marriage to Alex is binding. But convincing the earl will be another matter altogether. From what I hear of the man, he's prideful and does not like to lose."

"No Highlander likes to lose, Petro."

"What about you, Keely. Have you lost anything by marrying Alexander?"

She considered her new friend, then shook her head. "If I were honest, I would say I've gained more than I lost. I know Alex doesna love me yet, Petro. But it is worth the effort to win back his heart."

"You are very wrong, Lady Keely."

"He used to love me."

"Aye. And still does."

She'd reserve judgment for a future time. "What of the earl?"

"He wishes to see you."

"And Alex?"

"The request is to see you alone."

"Why? I am a married woman, and Alex willna let me

leave."

"I suspect he requires the same as your sire – explanation for why you left so suddenly. I will make the necessary arrangements."

His offer filled her with a determination to set things right. "Ye'd risk everything to do this?"

"If it gives Alex and you a chance at peace? Aye."

"Thank ye."

He patted her hand. "Do not thank me yet. If we are caught, Alex will never forgive me. But I would spare him this added burden when there is already so much for him to do."

"When will we leave?"

"After your father and brothers go home."

"That could take a while, Petro. My sire is slow to forgive."

"I will dispatch a reply to the earl."

Chapter Eighteen

"ARGUING ACCOMPLISHES NOTHING," Alex said, growing weary of Laird Oliphant's temper.

"Ye broke trust with me, Alex."

"I could say the same of ye."

The two men exchanged hard looks.

"The king willna approve of this unsanctioned marriage."

Alex dinna care. "By the time he grants ye an audience, Keely will be heavy with child."

"I am not leaving here without my daughter."

"Then ye will not be leaving at all."

Laird Oliphant grunted as he sat down in the closest chair and rubbed his temples. "The news of yer brother's death saddened me."

Alex took a deep breath. "The Sutherlands will pay dearly for it."

"Ye are no match for the earl."

"I willna wage open war on the man," Alex said. "But my brother will be avenged."

"Ye'd make my daughter twice a widow?"

"Does that mean ye accept our marriage?"

"I canna say yet. I am not a cold-hearted bastard—Keely's feelings do matter to me. More than anything, I want to know why she ran to the Sutherlands instead of coming home. I dinna have a heavy hand with her as a child. If anything, I spoiled the lass."

"Keely doesna need to be here to explain. The answer is simple. She tried to keep her word and married John out of obligation."

"What else is there? Our fathers took wives chosen for them. Romantic entanglements are for the young who doona have titles and lands to secure," Laird Oliphant said. "I commanded her to marry yer brother for strategic reasons."

"Father," Broc said. "If what the scholar told us is true, surely ye can appreciate Keely's reason for not coming home. Would ye have let her stay? Though I will never understand why she chose the Sutherlands."

"Of course not," the laird said emphatically. "She would have been sent back to her husband."

Alex knew there was no way to change the man's mind yet. It would take time. So instead of deepening the resentment between them, he decided to invite him to stay. "Perhaps the best way to see that our marriage deserves yer blessing is to spend some time here."

"Ply me with food and drink? Is that what ye plan to do?"

"I think it will help."

Laird Oliphant rewarded Alex with a toothy grin. "I like the way ye think, MacKay."

"Then it is settled?"

"Temporarily. Who am I to refuse eating and drinking on someone else's gold? My sons are gluttons, and so are my retainers."

"There is plenty of meat and bread on my table every night, Laird Oliphant—*Father.*"

"Doona get too comfortable throwing that title about, lad."

Alex would wear the old man down little by little, until he

had no choice but to accept him as a son-in-law. They left the solar together and returned to the great hall in search of Keely. When Alex dinna find her there, he sought out Mathe.

"Where is my wife?"

"At the loch."

"Is she all right?"

Mathe cracked a rare smile. "When I informed her that she wasna free to traipse about unescorted, she threatened to punch me in the nose."

"Aye?"

Mathe nodded. "I couldna risk it, Laird Alex—yer wee bride might pack a good wallop."

Alex gripped the captain's shoulder. "Ye made the right choice."

Things were far from settled between Alex and his bride, but while her father was in his house, he must be more lenient with Keely. He couldna fight all of Clan Oliphant and hope to win. He walked outside and headed for the loch.

He found her alone.

"I dinna expect to see ye alive again."

"Have ye so little faith in yer husband?" he asked, standing next to her.

"Tis not a lack of belief in yer abilities, Alex. I know my father—he's a temperamental sort, believes any worthy cause should be settled with fists or swords."

"A family trait, I believe," he said humorously.

"What do ye mean?"

"Ye threatened my captain with violence?"

"Aye. I dinna need him following me about."

"Yer escort isna just to make sure ye doona run away, Keely. I wish to keep ye safe."

"From who?"

"Sutherlands."

"And why would the Sutherlands wish me any harm?"

"Because ye're my wife."

Her blue gaze stayed on him as she absorbed his words. "I doona like to think that the earl or his sons would hurt me to get to ye, Alex. And I know ye hate them and have every right to."

"Desperate men strike without warning or purpose, Keely. Men of honor meet on the battlefield."

"Is that what ye think the earl is, desperate?"

"He is now," Alex said. "He must live with the uncertainty of when and how I will retaliate for John's death, and the murders of my tenants."

"Doesn't that make ye equally desperate?"

A fair question. Did it? Alex rubbed his chin. "Perhaps I am."

"There must be a way to avoid more bloodshed."

"Nay. I canna overlook what has been done. If I did, word would spread throughout the Highlands of how weak the MacKays have become. An eye for an eye."

"And whose eye do ye wish to take?"

"I willna settle for any less than one of his sons."

Keely nodded, but Alex dinna miss the worried look on her face. "Is my father ready to speak with me?'

"Aye—he's accepted my invitation to stay with us for a while. I wish ye to have some time with yer da, Keely, and yer brothers."

"And where will ye be?'

"Fortifying the west villages and recruiting new soldiers."

"How long will ye be gone?"

"Days at a time. But never too far away, lass."

She hopped off the boulder and smoothed the wrinkles from her skirts. "I doona wish to keep my father waiting. He deserves the truth."

Alex offered his arm. "I will take ye to him."

SURROUNDED BY HER brothers and seated across from her sire in front of the main hearth in the great hall, Keely couldna keep from smiling. Her brother Simon tugged on a strand of her hair.

"Ye're glowing," Simon teased.

"Tis warm in here," she said.

"Are ye happy, lass?" Broc asked.

As a child, Keely had been immeasurably happy. Her sire had indulged her, perhaps too much, because he felt guilty for her mother's death. Everything changed when she was sent to the MacKays for that first summer at the age of thirteen. Laird Oliphant thought it would benefit her immensely to spend time away from home, in preparation for when she would marry and be expected to run her own household.

Whether her da had planned it or not, Keely did fall in love with one of the MacKay sons. And Alex's father had always been affectionate with her, inviting her back every year. She looked about the familiar space and frowned when she saw the sheet again.

"What troubles ye?" Gavin, her second eldest brother asked.

"Tis nothing." She dinna want to ruin the moment.

"Keely…" His eyebrows arched.

"The bridal bed sheet is an embarrassment."

"Why?" Her other brother, Justice, asked. "The proof of yer purity is an honor to yer husband and all of us."

"I doona want it there," she complained.

"Very well." Broc yanked it down and balled it up. "If anyone complains, send them to me."

Keely jumped up from her chair and hugged her brother.

"Thank ye, Broc. All of ye. Father."

"For what, lass?" the laird asked.

"Coming here."

"Ye are an Oliphant. And we take care of our own," her father said. "But doona think all the pleasantries mean we've forgotten yer sins. What ye did was wrong. And I require an explanation."

Her shoulders drooped as she slipped back into the chair and faced her sire. "I am sorry that I disappointed ye, Father."

He blinked. "I am accustomed to disappointment, lass. With seven bairns, a man gets used to it. Tis the deception that's eating a hole in my gut."

"Deception?"

"Running off in the middle of the night instead of facing yer problems like a woman."

Keely folded her hands on her lap. Aye—she'd acted irresponsibly. She'd given up her heart's desire as her father had demanded. Her flight from the MacKays hadn't been premeditated. "I dinna plan to run away."

"Did John harm ye? Force ye to do anything? Curse ye?"

"Nay."

"Did ye feel unwelcome here?" he continued.

"Father," Keely started, eyeing her four brothers in search of support. "It had nothing to do with how I felt about Laird John or Clan MacKay."

"Ye're being deliberately difficult, girl."

"Nay. I just want ye to understand why."

"I've asked ye a dozen questions and am more confused than I ever was."

Gavin and Simon snickered.

"She's a woman, Father," Simon offered. "Doona try to make sense of it."

She leaned back in her chair, waiting while her brothers laughed at her expense. The years apart hadn't diminished the true affection she had for her family, nor had her siblings matured.

"I couldna face ye," she admitted, deciding to keep the explanation simple. Truth was truth no matter how she expressed it. Her body belonged to her, and as far as she was concerned, that meant her choice in husband should belong to her, too.

"Do ye have anything to be ashamed of, lass?"

"Nay, Father. Unless there's shame in loving a man." She watched her da for a long moment. Would he accept her reasoning? More importantly, would he bless her marriage, allow her to stay with Alex?

Laird Oliphant tugged on his beard. "Tis my fault, I shouldna have expected a mere girl to do a woman's work."

Finally, something they could agree on!

"I will have a full accounting of what transpired while ye were with the Sutherlands. And doona think the earl willna be held accountable. If I had taken his only daughter in without sending proper word, the man would have been banging on every gate in the Highlands until he found her."

"Aye, Father."

"Furthermore," he boomed. "Ye will promise to never run away again."

Just as she was about to swear, she remembered her earlier conversation with Petro. In truth, taking a secret trip to Dunrobin Castle would be considered the same as running away, wouldn't it?

"Well, lass?" Broc said softly.

"I promise." She couldna refuse to say it—her sire had required it as a condition for forgiveness.

"Tis settled then." Her sire stood and opened his arms. "As

for yer marriage, I will make that decision later. Give me a hug."

Keely was only too happy to embrace him again. She'd always felt safe in her father's strong arms—the same way she was beginning to feel about Alex.

"Now, where is my son-in-law?" Laird Oliphant asked much to Keely's surprise.

"In the bailey training with his captains," Broc directed him.

Once their father had left, Broc pulled Keely aside. "I am sorry for smacking ye, Keely."

She stared at the floor. Ten years older than she, Keely had always regarded Broc as the champion of their family. He was the future laird and very much like their father. She gazed up at him and the anger that had flared inside her when he hit her faded. "I forgive ye."

Chapter Nineteen

"SIX MASONS AND fifteen laborers are already rebuilding the cottages and the wall in the west village, Laird Alex," Jamie reported. "The extra hands will assure quick completion."

"Have ye taken an inventory for what we'll need for the other four villages? The same should be done—providing defenses so the next time the Sutherlands come looking for a fight, they'll get one."

"Aye. Accommodations for the guards are also being constructed."

Petro slid a ledger across the table to Alex. "I've finished the calculations, Alexander. There's enough gold to hire the necessary hands to make the improvements on the keep, build the second tower, and pay two hundred retainers through next year. But we'll need more money."

Alex scanned the parchment. Clan MacKay was luckily self-sufficient, yielding enough crops—oats, barley, turnips, and kale—to sustain the tenants. The storerooms were also well-stocked with preserved meats, butter, cheese, and ale. The cattle and sheep herds flourished. Fortunately, his sire and brother had exercised temperance when it came to spending money, sometimes to a fault. He dinna mind investing in his clan, using his own wealth to improve the lives of the people. But there remained one question: it would be necessary to send a representative back to Constantinople to settle his accounts and sell his property.

He'd considered several candidates, including Petro. But Alex dinna want to part ways with him. He needed his secretary to help run the keep and maintain a friendship with Keely. Mathe was a soldier and dinna have the disposition to deal with foreigners. But Jamie had a good head on his shoulders. And like Alex, he was tall and fierce looking and would win the respect of the lords in the east.

"There is something I wish to discuss with ye," Alex said to his cousin.

"Whatever ye need."

"Sit." Alex gestured to one of the chairs by the table. "As ye know, I dinna prepare for a long stay in Scotland."

"Aye," Jamie acknowledged, crossing his legs.

"I own extensive properties in Constantinople, employ sixty servants, own twenty slaves, and my concubines…"

Jamie coughed exaggeratedly.

"'Tis a delicate subject," Alex said.

"I never imagined ye as anything but a Highlander, Cousin."

"I am a Highlander first." Alex thumped his chest. "But if a man leaves his homeland, ye canna fault him for building a life elsewhere."

"Nay," Jamie said. "But I canna understand keeping slaves."

"Doona fash, Father Michael has provided the guidance I need to save my soul."

Jamie chuckled.

"It seems a man can be absolved of any sin as long as he has enough coin," Alex added.

"I'll remember it when I need forgiveness."

Alex rolled his eyes. There were stark differences between life in Scotland and Constantinople. Sometimes he still missed the heat and sand. But he'd willingly let go of that life and there was no going back now. "I want ye to sail to Constantinople."

Jamie leaned forward in the chair, resting his palms on the edge of the table. "Are ye daft? Leave home?"

"Aye. Ye've been to England and France."

"To advance MacKay interests, to fight for my laird," Jamie pointed out.

"And now ye will serve my interests by dissolving any ties I have in the east. I will pay ye a king's ransom, Jamie. Ye'll have enough coin to attract the kind of bride ye deserve."

His cousin dinna look convinced.

"What do I know of such a place? The people?"

"I will send Kuresh with ye. He will act as interpreter, councilor, and guide."

"What about Mathe? Or Gordon? He has a head for business—can haggle with the sellers at the market like an old woman."

"Aye, Gordon would be a wise choice, too. But he doesna have yer quick wit and sword arm. And he isna my kinsman. This requires someone I trust implicitly."

Alex had always lived with a sense of purpose, first for the honor of his family, and when his brother and Keely betrayed him, that purpose shifted to himself. Well, now it had switched back to family. And the wealth that would come from selling off his assets would make Clan MacKay a worthy adversary to the Sutherlands. Titles and lands were purely symbolic in Alex's mind. A man with enough gold to do whatever he wanted commanded his enemies' respect and fear.

"What about my seat on the council?"

"Name yer temporary replacement or grant proxy to one of the members. Yer place will be saved for when ye return. And trust me, Cousin, ye will come home." Alex could see the uncertainty on his face.

"How long will I be gone?"

"Two months."

"*An Diabhal fhéein*!"

"Doona incite the devil. Ask for protection from the Almighty if ye must," Alex suggested, attempting to hide his smile.

"Ye're not like other men, Alex. Nothing would make me want to leave the Highlands."

"Spoken like a man who has never experienced the kind of betrayal I have."

There was a long silence.

"Still about betrayal, is it?" Jamie asked sharply.

Alex clamped his jaw tight. "A subject better avoided."

"All right," Jamie said. "When do ye need my answer?"

"Now."

"Now?"

"Aye. The longer we wait, the better the chance of someone taking what is mine. I should have been on my ship weeks ago."

"Did ye no leave someone to act in yer absence?"

"Of course, a trusted servant who is trained to run my household," Alex said. "But there are powerful men who covet what I own."

"What if I refuse?"

Alex stiffened. "I havena thought that far ahead."

Jamie's eyebrows rose with surprise. "Ye say go, and I must."

"I am laird, and ye did swear fealty to me."

Jamie nodded. "It will cost ye, Cousin. I want my own lands. And a house."

"Ye wish to live apart from the clan?"

"Have ye not heard a word I've said, Alex? Our clan means everything to me. I would never leave. But I'd gladly take back what my father ceded to yer da before he died. Tis the price for my sword arm that ye value so much."

His cousin's demand wasna unreasonable. The voyage would take Jamie through pirate infested waters, so it would only be right to pay him. Alex still sought Petro's approval. Giving up land wasna something taken lightly. But Alex also recognized the importance of keeping his heir happy. If anything happened to Alex, or if Keely couldna bear him a son, Jamie would be the next laird. Another reason he wanted his cousin to take the trip. Nothing opened a man's eyes like Constantinople. He'd either find God or go to the devil.

"Five hundred acres along the sea coast," Petro said, referencing a map that Alex's father had always kept available. It showed the extent of Clan MacKay holdings. "A fair exchange for what you ask him to do."

"All right." Alex stood and walked around the table to where his cousin sat. "Ye'll have the land, and upon yer return, my masons will build whatever home ye want."

Jamie hoisted himself up to his feet, still looking unsure of the situation. "Two months?"

"Three, if the storm gods curse ye."

"Ye're a bloody pagan," Jamie said, clasping Alex's shoulder. "I willna fail ye. And once the shock of the moment passes, I am sure I will be grateful for the opportunity. It's just ... I've never considered traveling so far before. A man gets comfortable in his natural surroundings."

"We are creatures of habit," Alex agreed. "Some of them worse than others."

The two laughed, and Alex gripped his cousin's forearm.

"Thank ye, Jamie. I've always considered ye a brother."

Chapter Twenty

A WEEK LATER, as Keely dressed for the feast Alex had planned in honor of her father and Jamie's departure, she couldna help but feel a little sad. She'd miss Jamie. However, his quest filled her with hope. With Alex cutting ties in Constantinople, it meant he fully intended to stay in the Highlands. The fear that he'd secure his place as laird, get her with child, and then depart had always been in the back of her mind. Though they'd fallen into a comfortable routine lately, her husband showed no sign of softening toward her.

Aye, he treated her with decency and dinna hold back his passion at night. But she craved more—that intimate connection she'd seen other couples share. She turned and looked at Leah who was busy cleaning her dressing table.

"What troubles ye?" the maid asked.

"Nothing."

"I know ye're not telling the truth, Lady Keely. Whenever ye worry, crease lines appear between yer brows."

Had she grown that careless? While in residence at Dunrobin Castle, she had learned quickly to hide her feelings. Otherwise, the earl and his sons would question her, and Helen wouldna leave her side. Doubt whispered inside her as she tried to make sense of everything. Aye, she amused Alex and had proven herself an eager lover. But his interest in her seemed to end the moment the sun came up and he stepped out of their bedchamber.

She wanted more, to be his confidant and helpmate—to learn everything about managing Clan MacKay, inside and outside the keep. Numerous requests to accompany him on clan business had fallen on deaf ears. With other clans, sometimes the laird's wife settled disputes among the women, a duty she'd very much like to take on. It would ease his workload.

"Keeping secrets doesna help ye." Leah interrupted her thoughts.

"I have too many secrets to count."

The maid chuckled. "Tis only one thing that makes ye restless like this."

"Oh?"

"Aye—anything about Laird Alex."

Life revolved around him now. Even with her father and brothers visiting, she still felt half full. "I will simply have to accept whatever pieces of him he's willing to give me."

Leah clicked her tongue. "Ye'd give up so easily?"

"I've asked him to spend more time with me, to include me in his affairs." She felt defeated and had run out of options, with the exception of begging—but that would only make her husband angry.

Relief threaded through her when someone knocked on the door. Leah drooped her dusting cloth and wiped her hands on her smock.

"I will get it," Keely said. She needed the distraction.

Much to her delight, Petro greeted her when she opened the door.

"Lady Keely," he bowed. "Would you take a walk with me? I have news."

"What kind of news?" she asked curiously.

"The kind that no one else should hear."

She looked over her shoulder to make sure Leah wasn't listening. "I will get my cloak. Will ye wait out here?"

"Aye."

She closed the door quietly.

"Who was it?" Leah asked.

"I am going for a walk with Petro."

"But yer hair."

Keely preferred to wear it down. "There's still plenty of time before the feast starts," she said, choosing her best cloak and securing it around her shoulders. "If Alex sends for me, tell him where I am."

"Aye," Leah said, watching as she walked back to the door.

"The scholar is my friend," she assured the maid. "And those are in short supply here, Leah. Be happy for me." Keely slipped into the corridor.

"We will go out the back way," Petro suggested, taking her arm. "Your father and brothers are in the great hall."

"Drinking again?"

"Your father has a certain zeal for life."

"Aye, and once he starts drinking heavily, he willna stop until he falls off his chair."

Petro chortled. "We come from very different worlds."

"Yet ye chose to stay here. Why?"

Petro steered her through the passageway, then down a narrow set of stairs that led to the chambers where the maids slept. "I will not leave Alex. And the Highlands remind me of home."

She'd expected a more complicated reason for him giving up everything he knew. But it dinna matter, she wanted him to stay. He made life more enjoyable.

Impressed with his knowledge of the layout of the ancient,

stone keep, she couldna keep it to herself. "Ye've only lived here for six weeks, how is it ye're so comfortable with where to go? Do ye spend time exploring?"

"That's a nice way of saying it."

"Whatever do ye mean?"

Petro blushed! She couldna believe it. She'd never seen a man get that embarrassed before.

"Wait," she said as they stopped on the landing. "Only the women use these stairs."

"And I am not a woman."

"Nay, ye are very much a man." Keely tapped her chin in deep thought. "Are ye wooing one of the maids, Petro?"

The guilty look on his face provided the answer she needed.

"Aye. Her name is Glenna."

Keely knew the lass and her sister. "She's a fortunate woman to have attracted a man like ye."

"We meet at night, after everyone has gone to bed."

"Does Alex know?"

Petro nodded, and it greatly disappointed her that her husband wouldna confide in her.

"Come," Petro urged her to keep walking. "I do not want anyone to catch us here."

They turned left into another passageway, and ended up at a doorway that opened to the outside. The gardens were on this side of the keep, where the most sunlight reached. Once they were away from any people, Petro stopped and pulled a missive from inside his tunic.

"The earl has answered my missive."

"What does he have to say?"

"We are welcome at Dunrobin Castle."

Of all the things she'd done in the past, sneaking away to meet with the earl would be the most dangerous. Not that she feared for her safety. What she feared was Alex's wrath. If he found out that Struan claimed they were betrothed, he'd likely kill the earl's son and send her away to a convent. Nay, she must handle the situation on her own. And with Petro's help, she felt confident that everything would work in her favor.

"When do ye want to leave?"

"Tonight," he said.

She'd not expected that. "So soon?"

"Aye. Your father and brothers are distracted. Attend the feast as planned, and after we've eaten, I will challenge Alex to a drinking game. My cup will contain watered down wine. Once he is drunk, we will meet behind the stables. The horses will be waiting."

"May I see the letter?"

"Of course." Petro handed it to her.

Keely recognized the earl's dramatic script. He extended an open invitation, mentioned how much his daughter missed her, and offered blessings on the news of her marriage to Alex.

"These are not the words of the man I know." Keely looked up from the parchment.

"What do you mean?"

"The earl is a powerful man," she said. "He stops at nothing to get his way. I canna believe he'd offer his blessing, especially if his son wants to marry me."

"I will protect you with my life, Keely."

"I know." She squeezed his hand. "Perhaps my concern is misplaced. There is no reason for the earl to hurt me."

"If I thought for a moment we were in danger, I wouldn't follow through with our plan."

"And Struan must be silenced. I doona want Alex to hear from a stranger that I am engaged to another man, especially the earl's son!"

"I agree. The reward is worth the risk."

With the plan finalized, Petro escorted Keely back to her chamber.

"THESE ARE THE men who cursed my daughter?" Laird Oliphant gave the offenders a black look.

Alex had never intended for his father-in-law to find out what happened at the wedding. Unfortunately, one of Keely's brothers had been drinking with his soldiers. Too much ale brought out the worst in a man, made them gossip like an old woman.

"Aye. Their leader hasna recovered from my beating. He is dying."

"I want to see the bastard."

Frankly, Alex still wanted to kill him. But he'd not hurt a man who couldna stand and fight. Laird Oliphant might not be so honorable if he was given access to Levi. Nay, he must dissuade the laird. "Help me decide the fate of these men first."

Laird Oliphant studied each one. "That one isna strong enough to lift a sword. How old are ye, lad?" he asked the youngest.

"Fourteen."

Laird Oliphant grunted and looked at Alex. "A long stay in the kitchens working under yer head of household should chase the devil out of him."

"If that is what ye wish." Alex wanted his father-in-law to feel important, to have a hand in defending his daughter's honor.

"He's but a whelp, only guilty of doing what he's told. Where's yer da?"

The boy pointed at one of the other five men.

Laird Oliphant shook his head. "There's a special place in Hades for a man who would lead his son astray."

Alex signaled for one of the guards.

"Take the lad to the kitchens," he said. "Ye are to submit to Mistress Bradana. If word reaches me that ye're disobedient, ye'll get lashes. Do ye understand?"

The boy bowed. "Aye, milord."

As his father-in-law downed another cup of ale, Alex considered what to do with the other men. In Constantinople, all of them would be hung—a form of execution reserved for the lowest criminals. It had taken all of his strength to control his bloodthirsty nature on his wedding night. Levi's beating had been beyond brutal. But the punishment had to fit the crime. Accusing his wife of being a witch … that could cause trouble for his clan.

"Let my sons kill them," the laird suggested. "Broc needs a lesson or two about administering justice."

Alex placed his folded hands on the table. "Twould be within yer rights as Keely's father. Or mine as her husband. But I am afraid my wife wouldna speak with me again if she found out I ordered their executions."

"The lass shouldna have anything to say on such matters."

"She bore the brunt of their vulgarity."

The laird nodded. "What do ye think, Broc?"

Laird Oliphant's eldest son had a good head on his shoulders, so Alex was curious about what he'd say.

"If the leader lives, he deserves execution. But these five, I see the fear of the Almighty in their eyes. Ye canna risk another uprising. The whip will be wasted upon their rebellious hearts. Banishment is a fair punishment."

Alex rubbed his chin. Aye, sometimes banishment was a far

worse fate than death, especially in the winter. He'd be sure to send word to his neighbors not to take them in. All had families, and Alex would support their wives and children if they chose to stay.

"So be it," Alex said, pounding the table top with his fist. "The five of ye are forbidden to ever cross MacKay lands again. If ye're caught, ye will be killed on sight. Have ye anything to say?"

"I do, milord." Hamish stepped forward, wringing his hands nervously. "I have six bairns and a wife."

"Ye should have considered that before ye followed in Levi's footsteps."

"I was drunk, Laird Alex, caught up in the moment. Levi has a way of getting inside a man's head, using yer fears against ye."

"Look what that weakness has earned ye."

"Where will I go?"

"Away from here," Alex offered.

"Please, milord…"

Alex dinna want to hear anymore begging. He signaled for the guards, and they dragged the men away.

"I'll see that man," Laird Oliphant said. "Levi."

Alex stood and stretched. How could he keep Keely's father from going to the dungeon? Did he have a right to forbid him from confronting his daughter's accuser? "Tis a waste of time."

"Ye dinna hesitate to throw Keely in one of those filthy cells."

Jesus Christ. The tips of Alex's ears burned. "Consider the unfortunate circumstances of her unexpected return."

"She's a laird's daughter."

He must choose his words carefully. "And if ye'd been in my place, dealing with the death of yer brother and the aftermath of an attack from the Sutherlands, would ye not have suspected

Keely of being a spy? For God's sake, she lived with them for five years."

"Keely a spy?" The laird wet his lips. "I suspect it had nothing to do with her being a spy, Alex. But more to do with a broken heart ye've been nursing all this time."

Alex's jaw tightened. That hard truth hurt more than a sword wound. More than a burn. More than anything he could compare it to. "And how do ye know what I was feeling?"

The laird snickered. "Because a man of honor wouldna treat a noble woman the way ye did unless he held a grudge against her."

Alex paused and took a steadying breath. He hadn't expected an interrogation. But the man had every right to question him. He'd gone behind his back and married Keely. "Aye," he admitted. "Seeing her again resurrected some old feelings."

"I doona think those feelings ever went away, lad. And doona lie to me. I'm a father of seven and can tell when anyone is lying."

"She only spent a couple hours in the cell."

Laird Oliphant leaned back in his chair. "We are indebted to each other. I signed a marriage contract pledging Keely and her dowry to yer brother. She dinna fulfill her obligations. In turn, ye took something that wasna yers to take."

"The law…"

"Aye." His father-in-law held up his hands. "I've examined the documents yer scholar showed me. Ye've acted in accordance with the law, that much I canna deny. However, other things govern a man's heart and honor. Ye broke trust with me. Instead of bringing her home and presenting yer claim to me, ye acted selfishly."

It pained Alex to think of what would have happened if Keely's father had refused him and married his daughter to someone else. Aye, jealousy and possessiveness had played a huge role in his decision to rush his marriage. So had revenge. "I am guilty of everything ye say and unashamed to admit it. I would do it again if I had a chance."

One side of the laird's mouth tilted up. "I like ye, MacKay. That's why ye're still standing."

"I am fond of ye, too."

"Recompense must be made."

"Ye doona owe me anything. We are family now."

Laird Oliphant gave a humorless laugh and slapped his thigh. "Always jesting, lad. I meant *ye owe me* something."

"Ye have my pledge of loyalty, my friendship, and my appreciation."

"Gold," the elder laird demanded. "I want some of that money ye earned in Constantinople. I hear ye're as rich as a king."

His brows knitted together. The selfish bastard would squeeze everything out of Alex if he let him. "What do ye want?"

"That depends on ye." The laird stood up. "Now take me to Levi."

Chapter Twenty-One

KEELY SAID A short prayer and crossed herself before she stepped outside. The feast had been a somber affair. Alex and her father had been engaged in conversation all night, hardly acknowledging her or their guests. However, she couldna have asked for a better outcome, because it had given her the opportunity to slip abovestairs unnoticed, change her clothes, and take the back stairs outside.

During supper, guards were not posted outside her bedchamber. And at celebrations, unless the soldiers were stationed at the gates or on patrol, every man attended.

Leah had been harder to get away from, for the maid kept a close eye on Keely. She hoped her friend wouldna notice her missing gown. If Keely disguised herself as a servant, she had a better chance of getting through the gates with Petro.

As the scholar had promised, he was waiting behind the stables.

"Milady," he said quietly. "I started to worry. It is later than I hoped to leave."

"I left the feast as soon as I could and stopped by Leah's room to borrow one of her gowns. Mine are too adorned to pass as a maid in."

With a full moon overhead, she could see Petro's face clearly. He nodded and looked her over.

"Pull the hood up to hide your face. And if you are not averse to sharing the saddle with me, I think it best to ride through the gates as two lovers escaping to their private place."

A brilliant plan she wouldna have thought of herself. "I trust yer judgement," she said.

"Then we should go."

"Wait." She gripped his upper arm. "If ye have any doubts about accompanying me, please return and save yerself from any responsibility. I doona want ye to get in trouble with Alex. He cares a great deal about ye."

"Lady Keely," he said. "I am a grown man. If I did not wish to be here, I would have never offered to escort you to Dunrobin Castle. I am not deaf and blind. I've heard the gossip about you, and have seen firsthand how poorly some of the people treat you. Helping you is a duty I do not take lightly."

Tears filled Keely's eyes. She dinna know why exactly. Maybe knowing someone else understood how much she had suffered brought her a bit of comfort and the tears were out of gratitude instead of from sadness. "I am sorry for crying, Petro."

"Do not apologize for shedding tears. You are an exceptional woman."

Keely dinna take praise well, especially when she felt guilty. Petro boosted her into the saddle, then handed her the reins to the other horse. Once she was comfortable, he climbed up behind her and wrapped his arm about her waist.

"Try not to show the guards your face."

"What if they ask questions?"

"Let me do the talking. Are you ready?"

Her heart pounded like she'd just run up a mountain. "Aye," she said, resting her cheek against Petro's chest. She could feel his heartbeat; it was slow and steady. Did anything excite the scholar?

They reached the gates and one of the guards stopped Petro. "Where are ye going?"

Petro cleared his throat. "Away from probing eyes," he said.

The guard smiled. "Whose eyes?"

"The lass's father is inside the great hall. If he sees me with his daughter, he will geld me."

One of the other soldiers chuckled and said, "Let him pass—he's not a danger to us, only to himself."

"If someone comes looking for Katherine, will you deny ever seeing us?" Petro asked, playing his role perfectly.

Keely struggled to stay still, but she did.

"Aye. Yer secret is safe with me," the guard assured him as he slapped the horse on the rear. "Away with ye before I change my mind."

Petro heeled the beast into a gallop, and Keely lifted her head, watching as the keep faded into the darkness. Only after they'd been riding for a couple of hours did Petro dare to stop. He'd found a burn where the horses could drink.

Keely dismounted and took a shaky breath. "Do ye think we're being followed?'

"Nay," he said with confidence. "There is no reason for the guards to doubt what I told them. As for Alex, your sire, and brothers, I am sure they are still discussing what to do about the Sutherlands."

"Is that what has taken my husband away from me?"

"That and the need to gain your father's blessing for your marriage."

"Gods knows what demands he's putting on Alex."

"You have not heard?"

"About what?"

"Perhaps it is better not to say anything."

"Please, Petro. If ye doona tell me now, I willna be able to think about anything else."

The scholar started to pace. She'd never seen him nervous before. "Your father killed the man who interrupted your wedding."

The news saddened her greatly, for her sire had killed many men in his lifetime. Not that she considered him a murderer, for most had met their end on the battlefield. "This was one of his conditions in order for Alex to gain his approval?"

"Aye."

What next? Alex's blood? "My father can be uncompromising."

"Levi deserved to die, milady. And so did the men who supported his rebellion."

"How many were there?"

"Seven. One but a child. He's been placed under the care of the cook and the head of household."

"And the others?"

"Banished."

She supposed that was better than execution. Though it did surprise her Alex had let them live. For she'd never escape the nightmare of watching her husband beat a man within an inch of his life. Aye, she'd seen men die before from illness and sword fighting. But never from fists. That's why she intervened with Alex, asking him to stop. She'd been the cause of the unrest and felt responsible for the violence.

"You are very quiet," Petro observed.

"I am thinking."

"About what?"

"What will happen if we are caught."

Petro offered her a water skin. She took a long drink of the refreshing, cold water.

"Alex is unpredictable," he said. "I have seen him kill without conscience one day, and demonstrate the mercy of God the next."

"Let us hope we are caught on a good day then."

Petro laughed. "Are you hungry? I have smoked fish and venison, and some bread."

"I would like the fish."

He gave her a piece of cloth filled with meat. "Keep it with you on the horse," he suggested. "Unless you are more comfortable with me."

She'd never ridden at night before. And there did seem to be an advantage to staying with Petro. She felt safe. But she said, "I will ride my own horse."

"Very well," he said. "We should go then, I do not like staying in one place too long."

She'd travel all night if he wished it. The sooner she completed her business with the earl, the quicker she could return home. As long as Alex would take her back.

AFTER A LONG night of drinking too much ale and arguing with his father-in-law, Alex stumbled up the stairs to his bedchamber. He welcomed a good night's sleep. Keely had grown weary of the feast and retired early. Smart lass. It had taken a great amount of patience to entertain Laird Oliphant. Even his sons had abandoned them eventually.

The two guards posted in the passageway bowed, and Alex grunted as he opened the door. Not wanting to wake his wife, he unlaced and kicked off his boots. The warmth from the fire beckoned him, and he crossed the space as quietly as he could and sat in one of the padded chairs in front of the hearth. He folded his arms over his broad chest, rethinking everything he'd spoken to Laird Oliphant about. The one good thing to come out of their drunken revelry? A renewed treaty. The MacKays and Oliphants would stay allies.

Joining forces with the Gunns, Sinclairs, MacLeods, and if God willed it, the Keiths, the Sutherlands would have a difficult time attacking any of them again. It had been Alex's idea to organize mixed patrols. An equal number of soldiers from each clan working together to keep their borders secure. The men would work on two-month long shifts. Laird Oliphant would host a meeting with all the lairds at his keep as soon as it could be arranged.

"Damn the bastard," he said aloud, "he still hasna blessed my marriage."

Would his father-in-law ever accept it? Or maybe he simply liked keeping Alex guessing, for the man had a twisted sense of humor. And as for the payment he demanded, Alex would simply offer Keely's dowry back, though he hated to part with the land she brought with her to Clan MacKay.

He yawned and scrubbed his chin, his eyes as dry as the desert. The days and nights were bleeding together, lately. There had been so much to do, and still was. Enough men had been hired to construct the walls for the west villages, and several dozen new recruits had arrived in the last week. Good men, from what Alex had seen. Jamie would be leaving tomorrow. There could be no regrets about sending his cousin. He loved and respected him more than he had his own brother, John.

"And ye can rot," he said with a single tear rolling down his cheek. Aye, old feelings had resurfaced for his brother lately. Emotions he'd never admit to anyone but couldna deny himself. He blamed the ale.

Thirsty, he stood and walked to the table where a pitcher of water and cups were always kept. As he poured himself a drink, he gazed at the bed. He loved to see Keely's dark hair fanned out across the pillows when she slept. He liked to tangle his fingers in her silky tresses and get lost in her sweet scent while he thrust inside of her and made her sigh with pleasure. Maybe he should wake her up after all…

The bed was empty! He dropped his cup on the floor and rushed to the bedside.

"Fook!"

The guards banged on the door.

Alex hadna barred it yet.

"Graham. Neil. Get in here!"

The men stormed inside, took one look at him and the empty bed and knew immediately what to do.

"She takes the air sometimes," Neil offered.

"Likes to sit by the loch, too," Graham added.

"Where is Leah?" Alex seethed.

"I doona know, milord," Graham answered.

"Find her. Find my bloody wife!"

The soldiers departed, leaving Alex alone.

The ale-induced fog in his mind was clearing quickly as anger took hold. The lass had done it again. Aye, she'd fooled him, and tricked her own sire, too. She wasna taking the air at the loch. Not at this time of night. The guards at the gates wouldna let her through. His instructions had been the same since the day of her arrival. His wife must have an escort at all times.

Glad he hadna undressed yet, he grabbed his boots, shoved his feet inside, and laced them up. Keely MacKay would regret the day she was born—the day she showed her face to him again. Damn him for falling for it, for believing she'd changed, for allowing himself to care about her.

Alex left his bedchamber and went to his mother's old suite.

He kicked the bloody door open, knowing already that he wouldna find his wife within. Empty. He turned and started banging on every door, including Laird Oliphant's chamber. It took several moments, but the drunk laird threw the door open, his sword in hand.

"What is it, MacKay?"

Rage boiled over inside Alex as he stared at his wife's sire—a reminder of who and what she was. Without thinking twice about it, Alex punched the man in the face.

Built as thick as a tree trunk, the force of the blow only made Laird Oliphant angry. He rubbed his jaw and narrowed his eyes. "Are ye mad, MacKay?"

"Aye—a raving lunatic."

Keely's sire grinned and came at Alex. His meaty fist connected with Alex's gut.

Alex grunted and retaliated with a combination of punches. But Laird Oliphant was just as strong; he popped Alex in the mouth. Alex tasted blood, which only made him more determined to knock the fool out. This was his fault. Laird Oliphant had ruined his life by taking his daughter away from him the first time.

"Father! Alex! What are ye doing?" Broc wedged himself between them. "What is this about?"

Out of breath and shaking uncontrollably, Alex reached around Broc and boxed Laird Oliphant's ear.

"*Bod an Donais*!" the laird hissed.

"Ye're drunk idiots," Broc said.

Jamie and several of the Oliphant guards finally pulled them apart.

Alex fought to get loose, but Jamie and Broc held on tight.

"What happened here?" Mathe asked. "Did Laird Oliphant attack ye?"

"Nay."

"The bastard knocked on my door and struck me when I opened it," his father-in-law explained.

"Is that the truth?" Mathe eyed his laird. "Tell me it isna, please."

"Get yer fooking hands off me," Alex demanded, able to jerk himself free. "My wife is missing. Organize search parties. Find her."

The MacKay and Oliphant guards dispersed.

"Do ye have a hand in this?" Alex asked scathingly.

Laird Oliphant snorted. "If I wanted my daughter to leave this place, I'd not do it in the middle of the night like a coward. We'd walk out the front doors in the morning."

Alex clenched his hands, the urge to hit the laird growing.

"My father is telling the truth, Alex," Broc said.

"And why should I believe ye?"

"Will ye walk with me?" Broc asked.

Alex swallowed the bile in his throat and wiped the blood from his mouth with the back of his hand. "Aye."

"Father?" Broc gazed at his da. "I think ye should get dressed. We need to find Keely."

The old man threw Alex a disgusted look before he retreated back to his room and slammed the door.

"Never strike my sire again without cause."

Alex sized his brother-in-law up. The man had earned his respect and had every right to defend his father. Though Alex wouldna directly apologize, he nodded.

It was enough to satisfy Broc. "I know my sire is difficult enough to make anyone want to punch him. But he fully intends to bless your union with my sister."

"Then why has he waited so long?"

Broc shrugged. "He drinks enough ale to ferment his own

mind. I canna give ye a reasonable answer."

They could finish this conversation later. Alex wanted to find his wife. "Ride with me."

Broc gripped Alex's upper arm. "Aye."

They hurried belowstairs where a number of the guards had gathered in the main hall. Jamie and Mathe were busy organizing the search parties. There was nothing for Alex to do. He gestured at Broc.

"We can cover more ground alone."

Broc agreed and crossed himself. "May the Lord have mercy on us and my sister. Because unless she's been kidnapped, I'll throttle her myself."

Chapter Twenty-Two

THEY HAD CROSSED into Sutherland territory an hour ago. Keely knew her way to Dunrobin Castle, but in case she forgot, Petro had brought a map with him. It would take three days of hard riding to reach their destination. Though she was comfortable astride a horse, she dinna have the physical strength required to gallop over the unforgiving terrain without stopping often. The weather had deteriorated – the sun was hidden behind thick, gray clouds and a steady rain pelted her already soaked clothes.

Petro slowed his mount and waited for her to catch up. "Tis time to rest, Lady Keely."

"Not yet," she said.

The scholar gazed heavenward. "If I am a fair judge of the signs in the sky, this light rain is only the beginning. We should seek shelter."

Villages were located between there and Dunrobin, but the closest was still half a day's ride away. Caves and the occasional hut could also be found, but Keely dinna want to waste their precious time finding one. If the scholar could brave the elements, she too must try.

"I am willing to keep riding, Petro."

He refused and dismounted. "Your safety is my first priority. If anything happened to you, Alex would never forgive me, and I surely would not be able to live with myself."

His caring touched her heart.

"Climb down," he directed. "I will build a fire and we can eat."

She did as he asked, and followed him inside a copse where they'd take cover from the storm. She tied her horse to one of the trees and waited for Petro to build a fire. Keely liked to travel. The raw beauty of the Highlands had always called to her. Could any place be more blessed by the Almighty?

"Ye said the Highlands remind ye of home?"

"Aye," Petro said. "Not Rome, but my family's estate in the countryside. There's fields of grapes and figs. Vegetable gardens and fragrant flowers. The women go barefoot and bathe in the golden sunshine. The men wear sandals in the field at harvest time, their baskets overflowing with the bounty of the earth."

Keely tried to picture the place in her mind. "It sounds like paradise."

"Perhaps for another man."

"The memory of yer wife and son keeps ye from going back?"

"Aye," he said. "I buried them on our property behind the cottage and erected a monument stone with their names on it. I planted her favorite blooms… jasmine, crocuses, and violets, so she would always remember the happiness we shared. I spent months sitting by their graves, wondering what to do with my life. If I should remarry and start a new family. But my heart wasn't ready. And I refuse to wed a woman I do not love."

The man should be a poet, not a secretary. She swiped the tears from her eyes. "What I would give for that kind of love."

Petro finished building the fire, wiped his hands on his breeches, and settled beside her on the ground. "You are closer to it than you think."

"Are all Italians so optimistic?"

He grinned. "We are a passionate people."

"After years of war with England and constant clashes between the clans, the Scots have grown cynical and disappointingly practical when it comes to love."

"You are mistaken, Lady Keely."

"How so?"

"I do not know of another place that allows handfasting."

Keely shrugged. "There is nothing special about it. In the absence of a priest, a man and woman can declare themselves as married. It is an old tradition that many clans rely upon to secure treaties and preserve their bloodlines. There are those that take advantage and seduce maidens on the promise of holy wedlock."

"Nay," he disagreed. "In the heat of passion when a man desires a woman so fiercely and knows he cannot have her without making her his wife first – this is the sole purpose of handfasting, to preserve honor, to make the marriage bed holy."

Once again, his words astounded her. "I doona think ye're Italian, Petro."

"Nay?"

"I believe ye came from a faerie mound."

He chuckled. "I am too dark and ugly to be a magical creature."

"Ugly?" Toads were ugly. Insects were ugly. "Ye are a striking man."

Petro snorted. "And you are blind."

"Glenna likes ye."

"Aye," he confirmed. "I said I was ugly, not a bad lover."

He handed her a wineskin and she gladly took a drink—it warmed her insides. Then she ate a handful of venison and a piece of bread. As Petro had predicted, it started to rain harder and the winds picked up. She shivered and pulled her cloak tight around her shoulders.

"You are cold and tired." Petro unhooked his own cloak and offered it to her. "Sleep. I will keep watch."

"Thank ye." She could use a short nap. With the added warmth of his cloak, she curled into a ball and rested her cheek on her hands. She wondered if Alex had discovered her missing yet—if he believed she abandoned him again. If the man would only take the time to talk to her, to think about how easily she married him, that she'd opened up her arms on their wedding night and gave her body freely to him, he'd realize she'd actually chosen him as her husband.

She yawned and closed her eyes. There was time to worry about Alex tomorrow, after she settled things with the earl and Struan.

Sutherland territory

THE BAD WEATHER dinna dissuade Struan Sutherland from wanting to accomplish what he'd set out to do. Failure wasna an option. He'd been tracking the MacKays for over a week and keeping watch for any sign of Keely. His men were wet and tired, but there was time for comfort after they completed their task. They stayed in a camp just over the Sutherland border, a day's ride from the MacKay keep.

Just a mile away from his own camp, he'd spotted a fire while out on patrol. Many traveled this way and went unnoticed. And since the last attack on the MacKays, tensions were high on both sides. Struan knew the new laird would strike back at any time.

"I will ride ahead," he told his captain. "If they are MacKays,

I will ride back and get ye."

As Struan cautiously advanced, he recalled the exchange he'd had with his sire before he left Dunrobin Castle. The earl dinna love him, and Struan dinna love his father, but he respected him for the powerful man he was. And his future depended on his actions now.

"Ye're a worthless bastard," the earl thundered at his son.

Aye, *Struan thought as he waited for his sire to calm down,* I am that. *A bloody bastard who had high ambitions, especially when it came to Keely Oliphant. She'd all but promised to marry him—spending hours with him—laughing at his jokes—sitting next to him at supper—dancing with him on feast days—always smiling whenever she saw him. Either the lady had been stringing Struan along to secure her place in his sire's home or she cared for him. If the latter, he would do whatever he must to claim her as his bride.*

The earl shook the parchment in his hand. "We are expected to wait on the lady. She will visit us at her earliest convenience. And the missive doesna even bear her mark, it is the signature of the MacKay secretary."

Struan snatched the letter from his father's hand and read it.

The news of her marriage to Laird Alexander MacKay twisted his stomach with hatred. He'd never met the man before, but had heard enough stories to know him as a dishonorable sort. The kind of man Struan wouldna think twice about killing.

"Her dowry," his father continued, "more specifically, that fertile stretch of land between the Oliphant holdings and Clan Gunn, would have been tactically useful. More than ye know."

"I will bring her back."

"Oh, aye?" His father moved closer. "How?"

"Instead of waiting on Keely to come to us, give me a retinue and I will ride for the MacKay keep."

"Do ye plan on walking through the gates and demanding her back?"

"If that's what it takes."

The earl grabbed a fistful of his son's tunic and gave him a violent shake. "Fool. Do ye not know who Alex MacKay is? Where he's been?"

"Constantinople."

"Aye—fighting for the bloodthirsty barbarians. He's hard as steel, lad. Not pampered like ye."

Struan adjusted his collar. "If not a direct confrontation, allow me to spy on the MacKays, to get a feel for their daily routine. If I can take the lass, I will. And once she's back here..."

"She's been plucked and eaten," the earl said. "No longer a maiden."

Struan thought virgins were overvalued. Give him a lass who knew what she wanted, who could ride him, aye, he'd die a happy man. "I care little for such things. If anything, Laird MacKay has done me a favor by breaking her in."

His father frowned. "Do what ye must, Struan. And if ye fail, so help me, I'll regret the day I took mercy on yer life and claimed ye as my own."

Struan bowed and backed out of his sire's solar.

Though his father ruled his clan with an iron fist, he couldna control everything. The Sutherland holdings were vast, and not all of his tenants were as dedicated as they should be. Gold bought loyalty in the Highlands. And Struan had successfully organized a band of highwaymen three years ago. Robbing unsuspecting travelers was easy enough, and Struan had amassed a small fortune.

Politics hadn't inspired Struan to become a notorious thief. Nay, pure boredom had driven him to such extremes. Aye, he trained in the bailey every morning and could swing a sword and shoot an arrow as straight as any man. But he wanted more—needed more. Though his father's noble blood tamed him some, twas his mother's inferior family line that defined him. His maternal grandfather had been hung for piracy in Ireland twenty years ago.

As he reached the perimeter of the woods, Struan dismounted and walked the rest of the way. Two horses were tied next to the camp. There was no movement, not even someone keeping watch. He found two people sleeping next to each other. As he moved closer, the hairs on the back of his neck stood on end. He picked up a thick stick from the ground, opting for a club as a weapon instead of his sword.

That's when he noticed the woman and her thick black hair. Only one lass had those beautiful curls. *Keely.* He threw his head back and laughed at his luck. He couldna have prayed for a better outcome. She'd come back willingly. But who was her travelling companion?

Hungry to touch her and hear her voice, he accidently stepped on some twigs. The snapping sound alerted the man next to Keely. He shot up, a dirk in his hand.

"Who are you?" the stranger asked.

"Ye're on Sutherland lands," Struan said calmly. "Tell me what ye're doing with my betrothed?"

"You are Struan Sutherland?"

The fact that the stranger knew his name surprised him. "How do ye know me?'

"My name is Petro de' Medici, I am Laird Alexander MacKay's secretary." He reached inside his tunic and produced a missive with the Sutherland seal on it. "Your father invited Lady MacKay to Dunrobin Castle. I am her escort."

Why did he insist on calling her Lady MacKay? It angered Struan. Keely would be a Sutherland. His wife. "I will tell ye this only once. Keely Oliphant is betrothed to me."

Keely stirred and sat up, rubbing her eyes. "Petro? Who are ye talking to?"

The secretary dinna have a chance to answer, she followed the direction of his gaze.

"Struan?" she asked. "What are ye doing here?"

BY NIGHTFALL, ALEX and Broc returned to the keep. Their search hadna turned up anything. Keely was well away by now, and Alex felt crazy and helpless. If anyone got in his way, they'd suffer his wrath. He ascended the stairs into the great hall where many of his soldiers were waiting.

"Milord," Mathe met him halfway to the high table. "Did ye find her?"

Alex gave him a stern look. If his captain was asking him, then he knew none of the soldiers who'd returned had good news. "Nothing. The heavy rain likely washed away any tracks. My plan is to eat and pack enough supplies to last for a couple of weeks. I willna return again until I find my wife."

"I will go with ye."

"Nay, Mathe. Ye must stay here and take care of the clan. I will ask Jamie to put off his trip, and Broc and several Oliphant soldiers will accompany me south."

"I understand, milord. There is more to tell ye."

"What?" Alex claimed his seat at the high table and invited the captain to join him.

"I've questioned Leah."

"Does she know anything?"

"The last person she saw Lady Keely with was yer secretary."

"Where is Petro?"

"Gone, milord."

"Gone?" Perhaps spending time with Glenna?

"The guards reported he left the keep last night with a woman named Katherine."

Alex dinna know any maids by that name. He must check. "Bring Leah to me."

Jamie and Broc sat down with him.

"I rode west, Alex," Jamie said. "No one has seen her."

Why did it take Keely leaving again in order for Alex to realize how he truly felt? That he loved and needed her? That he'd never let go of the past—that she'd lived in his heart and mind for the last five years.

Alex had been an arrogant arse and blamed himself for her disappearance. While riding, he'd realized how cruel he'd been to Keely by isolating her, continually reminding her of how she'd betrayed him, denying his feelings, and keeping her under constant watch. What marriage could blossom under such conditions? Yet, she'd never faltered since they'd taken vows. Alex's insides knotted. He slapped the tabletop out of frustration.

"What is it?" Jamie asked, looking concerned.

"I've made a terrible mistake."

"Aye, ye have," Jamie said. "But it can be made right."

"Milord, ye asked to see me?"

Alex looked up and found Leah standing in front of the dais. She curtsied, looking as haggard as he felt.

"Aye, Leah. Is there anything ye can remember that might help us find yer mistress? A place she's mentioned, someone she's been spending time with?"

Tears filled the maid's eyes. "Nay, milord. She dinna feel well the night of the feast and went abovestairs. She asked me not to disturb her."

Alex turned a questioning look on Broc. "Did she speak with ye?"

"Briefly. Told me she couldna take listening to ye and my da arguing anymore."

"Laird Alex!" Neil rushed forward.

Alex shot up from his chair expecting bad news. His heart

plummeted. "What has happened?"

"We searched the scholar's chamber and found this." He held up a missive.

Alex rounded the table. "From who?'

"Yer scholar."

Alex snatched it from the soldier's hand and read it quickly.

Alex,

First, I ask for your forgiveness. If I did not think this a worthy cause, I would have never offered to take Lady Keely to Dunrobin Castle. A missive arrived days ago from the earl, accusing Keely of failing to honor her betrothal to Struan Sutherland. Upon speaking with your wife, I am convinced she never accepted such a proposal. The only way to settle this is to speak with the earl and his son in person. I take full responsibility for everything.

Your loyal servant,
Petro de' Medici

He read it a second and third time to make sure he hadna missed anything. "Fook!" He crumpled the parchment.

"Alex? Where is my sister?" Broc asked.

"Call back the men," Alex commanded. "Lady Keely has ridden for Dunrobin Castle."

"I doona understand." Broc followed Alex outside.

"Read it for yerself." He shoved the letter into his hand.

"I doona want to read it. I want ye to tell me why."

"Broc," Alex said while climbing onto his horse. "There will be time for questions later. Gather our men and ride southward. I willna wait on anyone."

He rode through the gates like the devil was on his heels.

Chapter Twenty-Three

KEELY TRIED TO spit the bit of cloth out of her mouth that the Sutherland guard had gagged her with. Her hands were tied behind her back and she was draped over Struan's lap. They dinna ride very far, for Struan stopped and she was handed down to a man while Struan dismounted.

"Take her to my tent," Struan ordered.

She kicked and tried to get away from her captor, but it dinna do any good. He half carried and dragged her inside the shelter, tossing her onto a pallet in the corner.

"There are no rules out here, Lady," he warned. "If ye doona obey, I will whip ye into submission."

She stared up at him, memorizing the details of his face.

A few moments later, Struan strutted inside and dismissed the guard. "Ye made it very easy for me, Keely." He hovered over her with a triumphant look on his handsome face. "Here..." He tugged the gag out of her mouth. "I am sorry for having to treat ye so rough."

Keely wet her lips and growled at him. "What have ye done with Petro?"

"Why are ye so worried about him?"

"Damn ye, Struan," she cursed. "Ye left him bleeding on the ground." When Struan announced he intended to take her back to Dunrobin Castle himself, Petro had attacked. But the scholar was no match for Struan. It only took one blow to the forehead to knock him out.

"All right, lass. I'll send one of my men to make sure he is still alive. Will that make ye happy?"

"Nothing will make me happy until ye let me go. But I thank ye for doing so. Petro has nothing to do with any of this."

"Firth," he yelled.

A man stuck his head through the flaps of the tent. "Sir?"

"Send one of the guards to the lady's escort. See that he's awake and able to travel. Escort him back to the MacKay keep."

"Aye."

"Ye see? I am capable of kindness."

"Why have ye taken me? We were on our way to see yer father, by his invitation."

Struan laughed wickedly. "If ye'd studied the missive a little closer, ye would have noticed the difference in the lettering. Though I am a talented forger, my father's script is more severe than my own hand."

"Ye're a bloody liar and a savage!"

He laughed again. "I always knew there was a hellion underneath that sweet smile. I look forward to spending more time with that side of ye, Keely Oliphant."

"Lady MacKay," she immediately corrected.

"Oliphant," he said, stalking closer. "Soon to be Sutherland." There was a flicker of something in his eyes that made her wary of challenging him too much. The look of a desperate man who would stop at nothing to get what he wanted. She'd caught glimpses of that side of Struan while living at Dunrobin Castle. But out here, away from the comfort and luxury of his home, it frightened her even more.

"Ye canna ignore the fact that I am a married woman."

"That dinna make a difference when ye ran away from yer

first husband, Laird John."

Keely struggled with the binding on her wrists. "Untie me at once."

"Nay," he said. "If ye prove ye willna try to escape, then I will consider it."

"Ye doona care about me."

"That is where ye are wrong. I kept my distance out of respect, Keely. But I know ye are no longer a maiden, which changes everything—for the better in my opinion."

She could feel herself blush.

"How endearing," he said.

"The shame I feel isna endearing, Struan. It should show ye that I am opposed to anything where ye are concerned."

He reached for her face, and Keely jerked away. But she could only retreat so far in the confines of the tent. He took another step and crouched down in front of her.

"Ye've missed the most important thing," he declared. "Ye are no longer in the MacKays custody. And whoever and whatever is on Sutherland lands belongs to the earl. And my sire..." This time he caressed her cheek. "Gave ye to me to wife."

She scoffed at his words. "The earl canna give away what belongs to another man."

"Damn ye," he muttered as he traced the arch of her eyebrows with his fingertips. As his hand moved down to her mouth, she waited until his thumb edged along her bottom lip, then bit him hard.

He screamed and shot up, shaking his bloody hand out like it would ease the pain.

Keely spat the piece of skin she'd bitten off on the ground.

"Ye little bitch." He slapped her face, but Keely dinna feel anything.

Her fear had turned into rage which numbed her senses. And if she ever got her hands free, she'd beat him to a bloody pulp. As long as she fought for her own honor, there was nothing Struan could do to hurt her, even if he raped her.

"I will forgive ye for that bit of violence, Keely. But if ye ever attack me again, ye will be very sorry."

She believed him.

"We will stay the night in camp. In the morning, I will take ye home. Helen will be overjoyed to have her companion back—her future sister."

She could scarcely think or speak at the thought of ever stepping inside Dunrobin Castle again. The place represented everything she hated, now. "Does Helen know about any of this?"

"What difference does it make? She's a woman and will do what she's told. As will ye."

"I am sure Helen would disagree."

He shrugged, and it infuriated her that he could remain so calm.

"Let me explain it in simpler terms, my sweet. Behave, and I shall reward ye. Cause trouble of any kind, and I will show ye how cruel I can be." To prove his point, he knelt in front of her again, only this time, he dinna touch her face. He lifted the hem of her skirts. "What are ye going to do?"

Keely sucked in a breath, weighing her options quickly. She could kick him, but then he'd beat her.

"Good lass," he whispered as his hand slipped up her thigh. "Aye—dear God..." He cupped her sex. "This belongs to me now."

She closed her eyes tight, picturing Alex's face—pretending it was his hand between her legs, anything to ease the mental agony of knowing Struan was touching her.

"Open yer eyes, woman," Struan commanded. "I willna take ye on the hard ground for our first time."

Relief washed over her as she dared to look at him again. "Where will I sleep?"

"In here with me."

"On the same bed?'

"Aye."

"Am I expected to sleep with my hands tied behind my back?"

Struan studied her. "That willna make for a restful night for either of us. I will send the guards in to make ye more comfortable." He started for the opening of the tent.

"Where are ye going?"

"Miss me already?" he asked, flashing his white teeth. "Doona worry, sweet, I will be back soon enough."

After he left, Keely tried again and again to break free. The chord was too strong and tight, and her wrists burned from the friction.

"Alex," she whispered aloud. "If ye ever loved me, please find me before it's too late."

SOMETIME IN THE middle of the night, Keely was awakened when someone grabbed her by the ankles and yanked her through the back of the tent. Though she wanted to scream, she dared not to. Whatever this game was, she'd not give Struan the satisfaction of knowing how afraid she truly was.

Once she was outside, she strained to get up, but the cloaked figure towering over her leaned down and covered her mouth. "Not a word, lass."

Alex? She nodded vigorously and he removed his hand from

her mouth. As if she weighed nothing, he scooped her up and carried her out of the camp. Moments later, he set her on her feet and used his knife to cut the cord about her wrists. As soon as she was free, she threw herself at him, and he caught her, holding her tight in his strong, protective arms.

"How did ye find me?"

He held her at arm's length. "Petro left a missive in his chamber letting me know where ye'd gone."

"Have ye found Petro yet?"

"What do ye mean, lass?"

"Struan hit him on the head with a club and left him for dead. I had to beg him to send someone to check on him. Struan promised he would see that Petro got home safely."

Alex frowned. "The man will pay."

Keely lowered her gaze to the ground, guilt and shame consuming her. "I-I am…"

She dinna have a chance to apologize, for Alex slanted his mouth over hers, swallowing her words. Desperation unraveled inside of her as she clung to her husband for dear life. The fear that she would never get to see him again, feel his arms about her, taste him, love him … it was too much to hold in. Tears trailed down her cheeks as she kissed him back, hoping in her heart that he'd forgive her stupidity, that he'd understand why she'd left again.

"Keely…"

"Alex."

"There's little time to sort this out right now. Ye're safe here. Hide in the trees and doona come out for anyone but me. I must finish what Struan Sutherland has started or this will never end."

"I understand, milord."

He tipped her chin up. "I forgive ye, Keely. But there will be recompense for yer actions."

She nodded, and would accept any punishment he handed down so long as he was the one administering it.

"Take this." He shoved something solid into her hand and then disappeared into the night.

It was a dagger, sharp and long and deadly. And she'd use it if she had to. As her husband had commanded, she found a hiding place under a cluster of trees. She held the knife with both hands, too scared to move or even breathe loudly. How her husband managed to find her and get her out of Struan's tent without getting caught or waking Struan, she'd probably never know. But she owed Alex and God a lifetime of gratitude and obedience. And she'd give it, so long as Alex loved her.

ALEX ENTERED THE Sutherland camp again. This time he dinna try to be quiet, he made all the noise it would take to rouse the drunks from sleep. He wanted to fight and kill every man he could get his hands on. No one stirred from their tents, so he picked up a discarded cup and started banging it against the rocks around the campfire.

"Come out and face me like a man, Struan Sutherland."

The first signs of dawn lit the sky. All the better, for Alex would look the man directly in the eyes as he buried his sword in Struan's black heart. To steal a maiden from her father's house was one thing, but to take a married woman from her husband–that crime carried a death sentence. No king or court in Europe would condemn Alex for having his revenge.

"Struan Sutherland!" he screamed for him again.

Finally, several tent flaps opened, and soldiers filed outside but dinna make a move against him.

"Who are ye?" one of the men asked.

"Laird Alexander MacKay."

"Jesus Christ," one of the soldiers muttered. "I told him not to take another man's woman."

"I willna fight for him," another said.

"He kept most of the gold we all worked equally hard to get last time," the first soldier added. "And now expects us to die for him?" He sized Alex up. "If we doona raise a weapon against ye…"

"I doona care who ye are or where yer loyalties lie," Alex said. "I have one man on my mind. If ye leave now…"

That's when Struan appeared on the other side of the fire, his sword at the ready. "How nice of ye to visit, Laird Alex."

Alex gave him an evil grin. He had never met the man before, but he hated him on first sight. Despised his slithery voice, his skulking face, even the way he held a sword. The way he hid on the other side of the firepit told him all he needed to know about the man's character. He was a coward. A true bastard in every sense of the word. So he'd die like a man without honor, not on his feet but on his back.

Alex dinna go around the fire, he ran through it like the devil himself, purposely loosing his sword on the way. He tackled Struan, who had no time to think or defend himself. The Sutherland bastard landed on his back with a loud thud and dinna move.

Instead of beating him, Alex slapped his face hard. When that dinna rouse him, he lifted one of the man's arms—it was limp.

"Bring a torch over here," Alex commanded whatever soldier stood closest.

"Aye, milord."

The torch was delivered immediately.

"Hold it above his head."

In the light, Alex found the reason Struan had been knocked unconscious. Blood stained the rock he had hit his head on when he fell.

"Is he dead?" the soldier asked.

"Nay. He still breathes. Bind his hands and bring him to his tent."

"Aye, milord."

Everything in the camp now belonged to Alex, including the Sutherland retainers. If they dinna swear fealty to him, he'd have every one of them executed. As he walked the distance to Struan's tent, men on horseback swarmed the encampment.

"Where is Alex MacKay?" he heard Laird Oliphant demand.

Alex grinned as he turned around and walked back to where he'd come from. "Matthew," he greeted his father-in-law by his Christian name.

The laird snorted. "Ye have bollocks aplenty," he praised as he swung down from the saddle. "Sacking this camp by yerself."

Alex lowered his head out or respect. "I had God on my side."

"Ye've suddenly found the Almighty again?"

"Somewhere between my home and this place."

"Good to know, MacKay. Bloody good to know. Where is my daughter?"

"Safe."

"And where is the bastard that took her?"

"Nay, no this time," Alex said. "Struan belongs to me."

"A kick in the ribs never killed a man."

"Yer kick in the ribs very well could."

His father-in-law chuckled so hard he coughed. "Best get my daughter. I wish to see her."

Alex wanted nothing more. He walked the half mile back to

where he'd left her, calling her name softly. "Keely. Ye can come out now."

"Is it over?" she asked, creeping out from the underbrush.

"Aye, Struan willna be bothering us again."

She ran into his open arms, and Alex buried his face in her long hair. "Can ye find it in yer heart to forgive a sinner?"

"What sins has he committed?"

"He's sure he's broken every commandment."

Keely lifted her head. "Ye coveted yer neighbor's wife?"

"No exactly," he said. "My neighbor's daughter."

That made her smile—that beautiful, delicate smile he wanted to see every day for the rest of his life. "I've killed, stolen, havena kept the Sabbath, and lied countless times."

"About what?"

"Ye," he whispered.

"Me?"

"Aye."

"Tell me what ye've lied about exactly."

Alex kissed her forehead, then her soft lips. "About how ye make me feel. There's so much love inside my heart right now, I think it might burst, Keely." He kneeled before her and took her hands in his. "I doona want to relive the past ever again. But I will tell ye this one time … I left the Highlands a broken man. And returned five years later still a broken man. Not one day has gone by when I havena thought of ye, craved ye in my mind and heart, in my bed, in my arms, in my life. And this time, Keely Oliphant, I am asking ye to marry me the right way."

He gazed up at her, waiting patiently for her to give him an answer.

"If ye doona want me, I understand. I know how many dreams ye gave up for me, for John, for my sire, and yer father. Men are swine, Keely. We doona consider the feelings of the people around us when we want something. If ye doona want to stay here, I will give ye my ship, and Petro and my men will take ye wherever ye wish to go. Italy. France…"

"Constantinople?"

That caught him off guard. But he'd decided to lay his world at her feet—whatever she wanted, she could have. "Aye, even Constantinople."

"Aye," she said. "I'll marry ye, Alexander. With all my heart. I love ye."

He slowly rose to his feet. "Say it again, lass."

"I love ye."

He tugged her into his arms. "I love ye, Keely. Always."

With the promise of a second chance at life with Keely in his heart, Alex carried his bride back to the encampment.

Epilogue

Two and a half years later…

"HAVENA I TOLD ye a dozen times ye canna go in the birthing room?" Laird Oliphant blocked the doorway.

Alex heard his wife scream for the hundredth time, and was ready to do anything to get through his wall of a father-in-law. "Get out of my way. Please."

"Nay."

"I asked nicely."

"I doona care if ye beg like a woman. Ye're not going in there."

"She's my wife!"

"And she's my daughter! But some things are sacred, Alex. And that birthing room is no place for a man. The pains will pass, the screaming will stop. My grandson will enter this world like a warrior."

Alex dinna give a shite about any of that. He wanted to hold Keely's hand, to comfort her, to take the pain inside his own body so she dinna have to suffer. "Move." He shoved the laird's shoulder.

Laird Oliphant laughed. "Ye shouldna have done that." He punched Alex in the face.

The pounding pain only made Alex more determined to get inside that chamber. He kicked the laird in the shin, causing the older man to hop one leg, but he still dinna budge from the doorway.

"Father. Alex." Broc had come abovestairs with Petro.

"What are ye doing, Alexander?" his secretary asked, shaking his head.

"This man…" Alex pointed at the laird. "Refuses to grant me access to my wife in my own house."

"Is that true, Father?" Broc asked.

Laird Oliphant nodded. "I've sired seven children. And not once did I impose on yer sweet mother when she was in the birthing room."

"Alex." Petro said in his soothing voice. "Perhaps a drink of ale? Some bread? A walk outside?"

Alex glared at his father-in-law.

"Yer nose is bleeding, Alex." Petro offered him a square of linen he pulled out of his tunic.

Another scream sounded, only this time, silence followed. A deafening, heart wrenching quiet that filled Alex with dread.

All of the men froze.

"Is she…" Alex started.

The cry of a baby broke the spell.

Laird Oliphant grinned and stepped aside. "Now ye can go in."

Alex would deal with the man later. He opened the door and his gaze instantly found his beautiful wife. She was propped up on a pile of pillows, and she smiled at him as soon as she saw him.

"Alex." She opened her arms.

He went to her and knelt beside the bed. "Are ye well, lass?"

"Aye. Tired but overjoyed."

"Lady Keely. Laird Alex." The midwife approached the bedside with a squirming bundle of linen. "Yer son." She placed the bairn in Keely's arms. "He's beautiful."

"Son?" Alex stared at his wife in awe.

"Aye. Our son."

He slowly stood up and leaned over so he could get a better look. Keely folded back the material. He had dark hair like his mother and pudgy, perfect fingers. Alex gently touched his head. "Milady," he said, gazing into his wife's blue eyes. "I am forever indebted to ye."

"Laird Alex," the midwife called.

What did she want now? Couldna it wait until the special moment with his family was over? "Aye?"

"Yer daughter." She offered another bundle to Alex this time.

"My what?" he said shakily.

"Yer precious daughter," Keely said. "Take her in yer arms."

Speechless, Alex cradled her, fascinated by her full head of thick, black curls. She stared up at him, her tiny mouth making sucking sounds. "Two babes?" he asked.

"Twins."

"No wonder ye were screaming to high heaven. I wanted to kill something because I knew ye suffered."

"Nay," she said, taking his hand. "It isna that kind of pain."

"I love ye, Keely. I love these bairns. This clan. The Highlands."

"I know ye do."

He repositioned his daughter in the crook of his arm and bent at the waist so he could kiss his wife. "Have ye thought of any names?"

"Rebecca, after my mother."

"A fine name," he approved.

"And our son?" she asked, arching a brow.

Alex had thought on it long and hard. He'd spent the last

two years of his life mending his ways, loving his wife, and forgiving his father and brother for the mistakes they'd all made. There was only one name that had stayed with him if he had a son. "John Matthew MacKay. After my brother and yer father."

"John and Rebecca," Keely repeated. "Worthy names for our little Highlanders."

"Aye."

"Now we better open that door, or my father and brothers, and even Petro, are never going to forgive us."

Alex did the honor, and when his father-in-law crossed the threshold, he placed the man's first granddaughter in his arms. "Rebecca," Alex said.

The Oliphant laird took one look at her and tears of joy filled his eyes. "Another Rebecca to love."

"And this is John Matthew," Keely called from the bed.

Her sire stared at her like she had two heads. "Ye had twins, Daughter?"

"Aye."

Everyone shuffled into the chamber, and the babes were handed around.

Alex stood back, taking in the happiness, grateful for everything God had blessed him with.

When Keely looked his way, he blew her a kiss. "Thank ye," he mouthed to her.

She smiled and nodded.

As he was about to join her at the bedside again, someone knocked on the chamber door. Since he was standing nearby, he opened it a crack.

One of the guards from outside bowed.

"What do ye want?"

"Sorry to intrude, milord, but Helen Sutherland is waiting at the gates."

Had he heard the man correctly? Alex stepped into the passageway and closed the door behind him. "Helen Sutherland is here? Alone?"

"Aye."

"What does the lady want?"

"Sanctuary."

Suddenly, the past he'd worked so hard to forget was staring him down. "I will go with ye."

He walked outside with the guard, through the bailey and to the gates. As the guard had said, a beautiful woman waited.

"Helen Sutherland?" Alex asked to be sure.

"Aye."

"I am Alex MacKay, Keely's husband."

Helen curtsied. "I know it is late, and I am sorry to disturb the peace in yer home. But my father is a raving lunatic, and I had to get away before he married me off to a decrepit and cruel laird from the isles. This is the only place I thought of—Keely is my only friend. There is nowhere else for me to go."

Alex considered it. Helen had been kind to his wife—providing what comfort she could when Keely's own life was in turmoil. And Helen obviously dinna want anything to do with her family, Clan MacKay's greatest enemy.

"Ye are welcome here."

"I am?"

He offered his arm and she took it, her leather boots crunching through the snow.

"Where is yer escort?" he asked, surprised the lady would be travelling in the middle of winter by herself.

"Escort?" she repeated as they stepped inside the main hall.

Alex ushered her to the main hearth and offered her a seat in front of it. Helen removed her wet gloves and leaned close to the fire, rubbing her hands.

"Not one man in service to my sire would dare help me. I am chattel, Laird MacKay, meant for one purpose."

"And what is that?"

"To increase my father's wealth through a strategic marriage. My heart and happiness have no value in my sire's eyes."

"What man did he choose for ye?"

"Laird Baran Munroe."

Alex's expression darkened. "No friend of the MacKays."

"No friend to anyone from what I hear," she added morosely. "Quick temper, and a murderer if the rumors are true."

"Aye," Alex said. "His second wife gave birth to a stillborn lass, and he starved her to death soon after. I am sorry for yer misfortune."

"As am I."

"Surely yer father knows the man's history."

"Aye. That dinna stop him from signing the betrothal contract. Though in my sire's defense, he made sure to include conditions for my protection—that Laird Munroe would never deprive me of food and water, or beat me to death if I gave him daughters."

Alex scratched his chin. "A generous concession on both men's parts, I am sure."

Helen laughed. "My father isna a bad man, Laird Alex. He's simply unfit to be *my* sire. I am to blame, too. For I have been too quiet and far too obedient all these years, leading my sire to think that I would do anything he asked of me."

Alex's sly smile reached his green eyes. "Keely wouldna love a lass so much who dinna have spirit."

"How is my friend?" Helen asked.

Alex rubbed the back of his head. "Yer timing is of interest," he admitted. "Keely has just given birth to twins, my son and daughter."

Helen jumped up. "Is she…"

"Resting comfortably and happy."

"Thank God."

"May I see her?"

Alex dinna want to excite his wife, not after what she'd just gone through. "In the morn," he offered. "After she's rested a spell."

"I understand, milord."

"Tis nothing against ye, Lady Helen."

She smiled softly.

"Do ye like children?" Keely would need help with the bairns. And who better than her closest friend?

"I adore bairns," she said sincerely. "New life is the promise of a new tomorrow."

He liked her words very much. "Are ye hungry?"

She nodded.

"Wait here." Alex walked down the short passageway that led to the kitchens.

The cook and maids were still working, but stopped as soon as they saw him.

"Laird Alex," the cook asked. "Did ye bring news for us about Lady Keely?"

Jesus, he'd nearly forgotten to share the joyous news. They'd all stayed up late because they loved their mistress so much. How things had changed since she returned on that fateful day two and a half years ago. It had taken hard work to win the hearts of his people again, to earn their trust back. Alex had given her permission to reside over the women's disputes every month, and she'd proven to be a fair judge. His household had never been more peaceful or efficiently run.

"Twins," he said. "John Matthew, and Rebecca. Perfect in every way. Lady Keely is recovering—she's a strong, lass."

The cheers were endless, and one of the maids handed him a cup of ale.

"Thank ye," he said, taking a much-needed drink. "There is a lady waiting in the great hall. She needs food and drink. Once she's finished eating, take her to my ma's chamber and give her whatever she needs."

The maid curtsied. "Aye, milord."

Alex offered his servants a last smile, then returned to the great hall and found Jamie waiting in the shadows. He was obviously transfixed by the golden beauty of Helen Sutherland and her black eyes.

"Jamie." He tapped his cousin on the shoulder.

"W-who is she?"

"No one ye need to concern yerself with. She is but a ghost."

"That woman is no spirit—she's flesh and blood, the bonniest I've ever seen."

Alex sighed. Damn his bad luck. "Helen Sutherland."

Jamie's eyes grew wide. "The Helen Sutherland?"

"The earl's daughter, aye."

"What is she doing here?"

"She asked for sanctuary, and I have granted it.'

"On what terms?"

"Her father made a betrothal she refuses to honor."

Jamie shook his head. "Tis always the beauties that get sold off to the ugliest bastards in the Highlands."

"She is welcome here for as long as she wishes to stay. Because she treated Keely with kindness and grace, I willna put her out. But ye…" Alex's expression grew serious. "Are to stay away from her. She is under my protection now."

Jamie cast a fleeting glance at Helen, then eyed Alex again. "Whatever ye say, Cousin."

Instead of leaving through the front doors, he stalked down

the corridor into the kitchens.

Alex knew Jamie wouldna stay away from Helen. For the last two years he'd tried to find a suitable wife for his cousin, but no one had captured his interest, until tonight. And that interest could cost his clan dearly. For once the Earl of Sutherland found out where his daughter was, the tentative peace they'd reached–after Alex returned his thief-of-a-bastard-son to him and explained how Struan had been robbing his noble guests on the road to Dunrobin–the treaty would be irrevocably broken.

So anything Alex could do to safeguard Helen should be done immediately.

He joined Helen by the hearth again. "I've arranged for food and yer room."

"Thank ye for yer generosity," she said.

"I will post guards outside the door to keep ye safe, Lady Helen. In case someone followed ye and wishes ye harm."

Alex knew the lady could see through his lie. He had every intention of keeping her in that bedchamber to protect himself and his clan. "Good night," Alex said, leaving her to return to his beloved wife.

Clan MacKay had enjoyed peace for two years, and he supposed it was time to shake things up again. He was always itching for a good fight. And just like Helen of Troy, Helen Sutherland had the face of an angel, the kind of beauty that could inspire men to kill each other.

That made him think of Jamie, again.

Aye, he must do whatever it took to keep him away from Helen Sutherland, so help him God.

THE END

The best way to stay in touch with Violetta Rand is to visit www.violettarandromance.com.

Subscribe to learn more about my books and to be the first to know about giveaways and sales.

CPSIA information can be obtained
at www.ICGtesting.com
Printed in the USA
BVHW040154200421
605383BV00022B/439